What People Are Saying About
Starting the Colt

Jan rounds up a good bit of knowledge and feel for life's lessons and the tribulations of a troubled young horseman in the Basin country. Listening to Fred and the "new" traditions of old horsemanship puts Ben squarely at odds with his father Pete's ideas of the "old" tried and true *cowboy up* and *ride out the buck* that he wants his son to learn. All the while, Ben's faced with the realities of dealing with life's lessons in loyalty, responsibility, family, and how we get along with people and horses alike. Although Jan's work is fiction, I can say that, coming from the background I have and looking back at parts of my youth, back in the day, "There's a whole lot of truth in the story of *Starting the Colt.*" A great read! —Smokie Brannaman, **author of** *Whisper This... Not to Your Horse, to Yourself* **and** *Equiknowlogy 101 (www.smokiebrannaman.com)*

Jan Young has written an authentic work, both in general and in the details. Her understanding of ranch life in northern Nevada is clear and true. Also her portrayal of the Lucas family is genuine and quite poignant at times. The adolescent struggles of young Ben are played out against a rich backdrop of a world where self-sufficiency and being a good neighbor are considered the norm. His youthful trials and tribulations as he strives to please his father and yet hold true to his own ideals are engaging to read. The author has not only researched her subject well but also has a clear understanding of the changing times with regard to working with horses on a cattle ranch. This is a very enjoyable read! — **John Saint Ryan** (*www. johnsaintryan.com)* and *(www.domavaquerainstruction.com)*

Jan Young's second novel, **Starting the Colt,** presents colt starting and horse training at its best. Twelve-year-old Ben Lucas faces a choice many colt starters must make—use the traditional method of breaking a colt or step outside of the box and work with the horse and learn its language. Readers also follow Ben through other adventures and anticipate the choices he will make to avoid getting into trouble. It's refreshing to read about rural life through the eyes of youth. Ben's work ethic and his ability to reason through his trials and adventures make him a good role model for readers of his age. Young's experience in Nevada's ranching community adds credibility and accuracy to her novels, which makes reading Ben's story that much more meaningful. — **Becky McGuyer**, high school journalism teacher and avid horse rider

I just finished reading *Starting the Colt,* Jan Young's exciting sequel to *The Orange Slipknot*. As I followed Ben's adventure I was especially interested to see how he would resolve his inner conflicts. I was pleased with Jan's conclusion. — **Milly Hunt Porter**, author of *The Horse Gods* and editor of *Think Harmony with Horses* by **Ray Hunt**

Once again Jan Young brings us Ben Lucas, the colt named Soapsuds, and life in the ranch lands of northern Nevada. Young Ben finds himself caught between his father, a hard riding, "ram and jam" cowboy, and old Fred, who is grouchy with people but gentle with horses. — **Jim Moore**, author of *Ride the Jawbone*

Author Jan Young returns to the northern Nevada sagebrush country to create a sequel which endears readers again to Ben, the ranch boy whose curiosity and enthusiasm can land him in tight troubles. — **Marcia Melton**, author of *The Boarding House*

Starting the Colt

by

Jan Young

Jan Young (signature)

Raven Publishing, Inc.
Norris, Montana

Starting the Colt

Published by: Raven Publishing, Inc.

PO Box 2866, Norris, MT 59745

www.ravenpublishing.net

ISBN 978-109378749-10-8

Copyright © 2014 Jan Young

Cover art © 2014 Pat Lehmkuhl

Printed in the United States

Library of Congress Cataloging-in-Publication Data

Young, Jan, 1951-
Starting the colt / by Jan Young ; cover art by Pat Lehmkuhl.
pages cm
Sequel to: Orange slipknot.
Summary: When cowboss Fred asks twelve-year-old Ben to begin training Soapsuds, Ben is caught between his father and Fred, two admirable men who have very different methods of starting a colt, and discovers he must find his own way.
Includes glossary.
ISBN 978-1-937849-10-8 (pbk. edition : alk. paper) -- ISBN 978-1-937849-11-5 (electronic edition)
[1. Horses--Training--Fiction. 2. Cowboys--Fiction. 3. Ranch life--Nevada--Fiction. 4. Conduct of life--Fiction. 5. Nevada--Fiction.] I. Lehmkuhl, Pat, illustrator. II. Title.
PZ7.Y86524St 2013
[Fic]--dc23
2012042548

Author's Note:

Be sure to use the glossary in the back of the book to learn about the many terms in this story that you may not be familiar with. Reading through the glossary will help you understand ranch and horse terms as well as cowboy slang.

Chapter 1

The school bus crawled away from the mailbox, shifting gears in a cloud of exhaust. Twelve-year-old Ben Lucas kicked his red ATV four-wheeler into gear and blasted down the dusty three-mile driveway toward home, the Circle A Ranch.

"Woo-hoo! It's Friday!" he yelled.

Rounding the last curve, he noticed some sort of commotion going on in the big roundpen used for starting colts.

Ben pulled up in a cloud of dust, killed the motor, and watched. The chunky sorrel gelding bucked hard, but Ben's dad spurred him even harder. A few more crowhops and their contest ended. Pete Lucas spurred the sweating horse into a half-hearted trot, its head hanging low in exhaustion.

A scrawny little man in a scruffy black felt hat leaned on the corral—Fred, the old grouchy cowboss on the Circle A Ranch. He was Pete's boss.

"Hey, Fred," Ben said, his eyes on his dad.

"Hey, kid," Fred said, nodding to Ben.

As they watched silently, Pete stepped off the lathered colt, opened the gate, and led him away.

Across the fence, in the next corral, stood a blotchy grayish-white gelding. His ears pricked up as he saw Ben. He ambled over to the fence, stretched his neck over the top rail, and nickered. Ben felt a knife twisting in his heart.

"So what do you think of this colt of mine?" he asked Fred.

Soapsuds wasn't really Ben's colt. But he *had* been, up until a couple of weeks ago. Now he belonged to the ranch. To Fred, more or less, since he ran things.

Giving up his colt—his first horse—had been the hardest thing Ben had ever done. He sighed. Oh, how he longed to have his colt back. How he wished he could go back and undo the foolishness of last summer.

"He shows lots of promise," Fred said. "I like his kind, intelligent eyes. I like his big raw-boned build. Pretty mature for his age." He hesitated, clearing his throat. "I've been thinking...he's about ready to start."

Ben frowned, fingering the key on his four-wheeler as he sat there. "Dad hadn't been planning on us starting him until he turns three."

"Course he wouldn't," Fred drawled. "He'd want him a bit bigger, stronger. I notice your dad's a bit, uh, hard on a horse."

"My dad's a good hand!" Ben said defensively.

"Now don't get in a huff! I ain't saying he's not," the weathered old man said. "He's my best hand."

Fred spit in the dirt. "I start my colts a little easier. Each cowboy's got his own way. I can start them when they're younger. I'm not as big a man as your dad."

That's for sure, thought Ben with a silent laugh,

eyeballing the scrawny, bony little wisp of a man. As his dad said, one good fart and he'd blow away in the wind. Ben pictured that in his mind, holding back a chuckle.

"He'll be three in the spring. It's only October," Ben said. "Of course, he's your horse now," he added bitterly.

"Yep," Fred answered. "Well, he's a long two-year-old, so I'd start him this fall, put thirty rides on him, and turn him out till next year, let him grow up. When he's three, we'll start putting him to work."

Narrowing his eyes, he looked the colt over. "I'm thinking I came out slicker than a whistle on this deal. Old Soapy here..."

"Soapsuds," Ben interrupted, correcting him.

"Whatever. He looks to be a lot better horse than that old yellow gelding you sent to horse heaven."

Ben reddened. "I didn't kill him!" he said, his voice rising. "You put him down because he broke his leg!"

"And who was responsible for him getting loose and running off so he could break his leg?" Fred demanded.

Ben clenched his jaw. Sometimes Fred made him so mad. The two of them got along better now, ever since that day on the mountain a few weeks ago. But that didn't change the fact that Fred was just plain grouchy and hard-headed. And why couldn't he let bygones be bygones? Ben bit his lip and decided he'd best not say any more.

"Come here, kid." Fred leaned both arms on the top rail of the fence and nodded his head to the side.

Ben swung his leg over the big padded seat and got up, feeling sullen. He joined Fred. *Now what?* Fred was probably going to chew him out for something stupid he'd done. He tried to think of what it might be this time.

Fred didn't speak for a long while. Then he said, "There're not many true buckaroos left...true horsemen that know the old ways...the art of horsemanship. Did you know my family goes clear back to the vaqueros? Back in *Cal-i-for-nee-uh*." He emphasized each syllable. "Back before my kinfolk came here to Nevada in the silver mining days."

Ben noticed Fred's dark complexion. So he had some Spanish blood. Ben knew a little about the history of the Spanish vaqueros who came from Mexico to California. "Yep. The art of handling horses has been passed down from father to son for many a generation." He sighed and paused. "I got me no son."

Ben swallowed hard and glanced over at the barn where his dad was brushing down the sweaty colt tied at the hitching rail. He knew about the son Fred once had... about the accident that took his wife and nine-year-old boy...the boy that Ben reminded him of. Fred even showed Ben his picture—the same reddish-blond hair, serious blue eyes, scattered freckles. The day Fred told him the story marked the beginning of their new friendship.

"I've been thinking," Fred said. "I got this here colt that needs started. I'm getting to be an old man. And I know you got a hankering to ride him." He turned and looked straight at Ben.

Ben's heart beat faster.

"And now that we're friends and all..."

His eyes bore into Ben. Finally he said awkwardly, "I guess what I'm trying to say is, I'd like to teach you what I know. Would you want to help me start him?"

Ben gulped hard. Wildfire raced through his body. Ride Soapsuds? It would almost be like having him back again! His heart pounded, doing flip-flops, jumping back and forth between his stomach and his throat.

But it wouldn't do to carry on in front of Fred like a little kid. He couldn't jump up and down and yell "Yippee!" even though he felt like it. After all, he was twelve years old—almost a man.

He stared at the ground, his lips twitching, trying to compose an answer. Finally he turned to Fred. Steadying his voice, he said, "If you think you can stand to have me around that much, I'd sure like to help start him."

Fred considered that answer. "Well," he drawled, "you can be kind of owl-headed sometimes. But...I wouldn't have offered if I didn't think I could stand you."

They both grinned. Not too long ago Fred had told him that he never wanted to see Ben around his horses again. They had hated each other. How things had changed.

"You got a little time right now?"

Ben nodded and jumped on his four-wheeler. "Let me just change clothes and grab a snack and my boots." He revved the motor.

"I'll be right back!" he yelled over his shoulder as he blasted down the dirt road to his house, half a mile farther past the barn.

"Oh, my colt, my colt!" he breathed as he rode.

Chapter 2

In ten minutes Ben returned, still chewing a mouthful of cookie. A saddled black gelding stood waiting in the corral. Fred picked up the reins and stepped easily into the saddle. Turning off his motor, Ben sat watching, his cap shading his eyes from the late afternoon sun.

Fred leaned on the wide flat saddle horn, his forearms crossed, the slack reins dangling loosely from the fingers of his left hand.

"The main thing," he began, "is to take your time. Start them slow." He fingered his reins absently and looked down at his horse.

"Old Black Bob here is six, and I've only been riding him in the spade bit for a year now. The vaqueros started their horses slow and gentle. They started them in a bosal." Fred pronounced it with a slow drawl: "bow-zal." "But today we often start them in the snaffle, for maybe a year or two. Then we put them in the bosal, for maybe another year or two. It works on their nose and jaw. Keeps their mouth light and soft for the bit later on."

He straightened up. Black Bob came to attention, his ears moving back and forth. Although the reins hung slack, the horse backed up eight or ten steps.

Ben laughed out loud. "How did you do that?" he asked. "Magic or something?"

Fred didn't answer but looked down at Ben with mild amusement. Now his horse pivoted to the left, stopped, pivoted to the right, backed up, and then stepped forward again. Fred watched his reaction.

Ben's mouth hung open. "But...you didn't even use your reins, or your spurs! You didn't even move!"

"The vaqueros ride a horse with lots of slack in the reins," Fred explained. "You don't pull or yank. You signal him with your body—your seat and legs."

Without shortening his reins, he broke Black Bob right out into a soft lope, rode a couple small circles around Ben, and slid his horse to a stop.

Ben shook his head in amazement. "Will Soapsuds be able to do that?" he asked excitedly.

"In time," Fred answered. "If you're patient and careful. Black Bob didn't start out like this. But you gotta learn to stop that rammin' and jammin'."

"Huh?" Ben said.

"That's the way you and your dad ride. Ram and jam, yank and spur. Don't get me wrong—he's good with a horse, and he knows cattle. He dang sure gets the job done. But...he's got no fin-ESSE." He emphasized the word, drawing it out while raising his wild gray and black eyebrows and pulling the corners of his mouth wider.

Ben thought it sounded funny coming from Fred. He whispered it to himself, imitating Fred's face.

"How do you mean...finesse?" he asked.

"He's got no smooooooth," Fred explained, puckering his lips and making it rhyme with "tooth."

Ben silently laughed. *Maybe Fred should try some of that* fin-esse *when he combs his hair.*

"Here, get on him."

As Fred swung down from the saddle, Ben jumped off the four-wheeler and crawled through the fence. Hitching up his pants, he grabbed the smooth braided rawhide reins and climbed into the saddle. When he gathered his reins snugly, he immediately felt the horse tighten. Black Bob's head went up and he pinned his ears.

"What's wrong with him?" Ben asked.

"Give him slack! You can't ride a spade bit with a tight rein." Ben loosened his reins.

"More! Throw him the slack!" Ben gave him more. The reins now dangled loosely.

"But now I haven't got a hold of him," Ben protested. "What if he tries to take off or something?"

"He won't."

"But what if he does?"

"He won't! That's why you don't put a spade bit on a green horse," Fred explained. "This gelding ain't exactly finished, but he's fairly ed-u-ca-ted." Fred pronounced the word slowly. "He'll stand until you tell him to move his feet."

Ben looked doubtful.

"Shift your weight back, just a little. Tighten your legs, just a tad." The horse responded by moving back a few steps.

Ben's mouth dropped open again. "Ha!"

"Walk him off."

He kicked him in the sides, and Black Bob almost jumped out from under him. Ben grabbed leather, his face burning.

"Whoa!" yelled Fred. "No ram and jam! Just shift your weight forward and suggest he move off."

This time the horse moved off softly.

"Now turn your head and look over your left shoulder at the barn."

Ben obeyed, looking around. The horse pivoted swiftly to the left. Ben grabbed leather again to keep from losing his seat.

"Wow! How did he do that?"

Fred grinned. "He's following your body. You had to turn your body to look over there."

Ben spent the next half-hour getting a riding lesson. He had never felt a horse as responsive as Fred's black gelding.

"Makes your butt giggle, doesn't it?" commented Fred as Ben reluctantly dismounted. "Be here in the morning. Eight o'clock."

Ben drove home, giddy with happiness. He tried to digest this new way of thinking about horses.

"Dinner's ready," Ben's mother announced as he walked in. Susie Lucas's short bouncy hair was strawberry blond like Ben's.

"How did that colt go today?" she asked Pete as they sat down.

"Oh, he was kind of a knucklehead, but I showed him who was boss. Pass the gravy, would you?" he asked as he scooped some mashed potatoes.

"I hope he didn't buck you off," she said with concern. "I don't see you limping. Ben, have some broccoli."

Ben made an impatient face as he took a small spoonful. *I wish they'd quit talking so I could tell about Soapsuds.*

"Well, he tried me pretty hard, but he ran out of air. I've always been pretty good at bucking out a colt!"

Susie shook her head. "I worry about you getting bucked off and hurt."

Pete nodded his head toward Ben as he took a big bite of roast beef. With his mouth full, he said, "I picked up a couple of nice colts at that sale last week." He swallowed. "Might be one suitable for Ben. He's needing a colt to start. I'm thinking I'll have him buck them out."

Ben sat bolt upright, all ears. *A colt? For me?*

Susie shook her head. "Oh, honey, he might get hurt! He's so young."

"Mom! I'm not a kid anymore," Ben protested.

"But, Pete!" Susie argued, ignoring Ben.

"He's old enough to buck out some colts. Aren't you, pardner?" he asked Ben with a wink.

The thought of being slammed into the ground by a snorting, stomping, unbroke horse gave Ben the heebee-jeebies. But he ached for a colt of his own.

Avoiding his dad's question, he said, "Dad, guess what! Fred's going to let me help him start Soapsuds! On

Saturday!"

Pete looked surprised.

"And he's going to teach me a bunch of neat stuff about horses and horsemanship and how the vaqueros rode."

"Huh?"

"But he says I got to learn to stop ramming and jamming," Ben blurted. "He says I ride just like you."

As soon as the words left his mouth, Ben realized what he'd just said. Heat crawled up his neck. *Stupid, stupid me! When will I learn to think before I open my big fat mouth?*

Pete's coffee cup stopped in mid-air. "Oh, he did, now did he? What's that supposed to mean?"

Ben cringed at his dad's tone of voice. He tried to cover his poor choice of words with more words, quickly adding, "He let me ride Black Bob. He moved like magic! Oh Dad, it was so cool! It was like riding a cloud."

Pete did not share Ben's excitement. "I taught you to ride just fine."

"I know, Dad. But Fred showed me stuff I never even thought of. I want to ride like that. I want Soapsuds to feel like that!"

Pete laid his knife and fork down on the table, his face stern. His eyes, as blue as Ben's, turned cold.

"Listen, Ben," he said slowly. "There are COW-boys, and then there are HORSE-boys." His voice held a sneer. "Horse-boys are always dinging with their horses, like they're some kind of fine china or something. But cowboys get the job done. A horse is just a tool. Don't let Fred fill your head with a bunch of nonsense."

Ben shook his head. "But Dad, Fred says..."

"*Fred says this...and Fred says that,*" Pete mimicked sarcastically. His eyes glinted like steel.

Ben bit his lip and looked down. *Why does he have to be like that?*

He glanced at his mother. Susie shrugged her shoulders and shook her head.

Why can't Dad understand how I feel? I always thought he loved horses. He stared at his plate, sighed, and slowly began to eat his dinner.

Ben idolized his dad. He had always wanted to be just like him—a cowboy, a cowman, a man's man. He tried to focus the images in his mind—Pete, Fred, Black Bob, Soapsuds, the sorrel colt in the roundpen—but they only blurred. Dinner seemed tasteless, and he left the table without asking about dessert.

Chapter 3

Early Saturday morning, Ben jumped out of bed, ready for the big day. *I'm going to ride Soapsuds today!* His head floated so far up in the clouds, his feet seemed to barely touch the floor.

"Fred and I are going to start my colt today!" he reminded his dad at the breakfast table, his voice cracking. *Darn! I hate that, especially when I'm talking to my dad!*

He caught his dad's annoyed look. Pete squinted his eyes a little. "*Your* colt?"

Ben tried to use his lowest voice so it wouldn't crack again. "Well, I know he's not *my* colt, but...you know what I mean..."

"Just buck him out. I want to see how you handle a bronc," Pete said, putting on his hat and jacket. "You've got to start practicing for high school rodeo. Just a couple years away, you know."

"But Fred said that's not the way..." Ben's voice trailed off as Pete slammed the door on his way out. Ben sighed.

"Why do I have to ride broncs just because Dad did?" he complained to his mom.

"You don't want to?" she asked. "I hope you don't. It scares me."

"I don't know," Ben answered. But he did know. He was afraid. "I don't want to disappoint Dad. He'll think I don't have any guts."

"Oh, phooey. As if that is the most important thing in life," Susie said with a snort.

"Well, Dad thinks so." He sighed. "I know he thinks I'm not very tough. I can tell by the way he talks to me sometimes."

"Nonsense," his mom said. "What do you think?"

Ben frowned. "I don't know. Maybe I'm not."

Susie tousled his hair and laughed.

"Men!" she said with exasperation. "You all worry about the strangest things!"

Ben pushed her hand away, annoyed. "You just don't get it, Mom." His voice cracked again.

He left the house early enough to do his chores before meeting Fred at the barn at eight. He took the trash out to the burn barrel and lit it, covering it with the wire screen to keep sparks from escaping. Safety was important, living an hour away from Elko's fire trucks. But their little town of Greeley, only 15 miles away, would have a truck soon.

He drove his four-wheeler down the road away from the barn to the pasture where his dad kept his bay gelding and his old white mare. Ben loved riding his ATV, a present from his rich grandparents in California.

His computer was also a gift from them—his parents couldn't afford stuff like that. His grandparents thought these things would help him be more like kids in the "real world," since they thought he was growing up so far from civilization.

He heaved upward on the stiff handle of the frost-free faucet and started the water flowing in the big round aluminum tank. While it splashed noisily, he picked up a two-by-four lying in the weeds and smashed the ice. On the high desert, fall nights often fell well below freezing. Snow blanketed the Ruby Mountains that towered over the valley.

Ben grabbed a few flakes of hay from the small stack of bales and tossed them over the barb wire fence. One for Whitey, one for Bones. The crackly-soft hay smelled sweet and fragrant.

Ben had learned to ride on old Whitey. When her last colt, Soapsuds, was born, Ben's dad decided it was time for him to have his own colt to start.

These horses carried his dad's brand on their right shoulder: "P" with an upside-down "L" attached to the bottom right side of the "P." Each cowboy was assigned a half dozen of the ranch's horses—his own private string—but most also owned at least one or two.

Soapsuds had lived in this pasture until a couple of weeks ago. Now he belonged to the ranch, but he wasn't on anyone's string...yet.

Ben turned off the water and headed for the barn as Fred's pickup pulled up. In his excitement, he couldn't keep from speeding. Fred got out as Ben pulled up beside him.

"G'morning!" Ben called, his chest about to burst.

"Ain't you got any brakes on that thing?" Fred growled.

"I've *told* you not to drive that fast in the yard. You just kick up a bunch of dust."

"Sorry." Ben's stomach quivered. This was *not* the time to make Fred mad.

"I got them yearling colts in that pen over there. We're going to mess with them a little today."

"You mean, before we start Soapsuds?" Ben asked, surprised.

"We ain't starting him today," Fred said roughly. "You need to learn some things first. I'll see how you follow directions." He spit in the dirt. "If you do alright helping me with them babies, we'll start messing with the colt one of these days."

Ben's heart fell like a sack of wet manure. Thunk!

It's not fair! he screamed inside. *I thought I was riding him today! This is the day I've been dreaming of!* He chewed hard on his lip and gulped. *I won't cry. I'm too big for that.*

He dared not argue, having already scored one black mark this morning. Had Fred changed his plan at the last second because he was mad about Ben speeding? Or had this been his plan all along? He could swear Fred said they'd start the colt Saturday. Then again, maybe he had just assumed that's what Fred meant.

Ben felt guilty. *I should be happy that Fred is letting me help him with the horses. I could BE happy, if he had only told me the deal.* He swallowed hard and tried to make his face look normal, but it felt like a mask.

While Fred ran a little roan filly into the pen down the alley and into the roundpen, Ben held the gate, fighting off the desire to just quit and go home. He couldn't let his anger and hurt feelings show. Fred would be watching to see how he did today. With a deep breath, he resolved to do his best.

While Ben shut the gate, Fred picked up a coiled lass rope and moved to the center of the pen, shaking out a loop and taking a few swings.

The filly galloped around the pen, snorting and shaking her head. With a flick of his wrist, Fred sent the loop sailing, and it settled around her neck. He let her continue running around the pen.

Ben leaned on the fence, watching. He wondered what Fred would have him do.

"I'll just let her wear this a minute," Fred explained, standing in the middle and turning as she circled him. "I'm just looking for a change in her attitude."

"How do you know what her attitude is?" Ben asked.

Fred continued turning, his eyes never leaving the young horse. "See how high her head is, see her looking to the outside of the roundpen? She's looking for the exit sign. See her tail up, her hard neck muscles, her tight jaw?"

Ben looked. All he noticed was a horse running around wearing a rope. He looked harder, trying to see what Fred saw.

"There. She snuck a peek at me. Did you see that?"

For a second, Ben thought about lying so Fred would think he actually saw it. "No," he answered honestly. Everything looked just the same to him.

"Her left ear flicked toward me for just a second, and

then her eye," Fred explained. "She's getting ready to slow her feet down."

"How do you know that?" Ben asked.

"Her body language. She's telling me."

Still watching the filly, Fred explained, "You have to learn to *see*. She tells you when she's tense or when she's relaxed. There, did you see a change?"

Ben looked hard. Something was different about the way the horse moved. He couldn't say just what.

"Sorta...maybe."

"Her eye softened, her head dropped a couple inches, her jaw's not clamped anymore, and her feet slowed down a tad. Hear that slower beat?"

Ben tried to see and hear those things. He wasn't sure.

"Keep watching. I'll tell you."

The roan dropped to a trot, then a walk.

"See her head coming down? She's got to relax her neck to lower her head."

Ben could see that the roan glanced at Fred. "Her ears are forward now," he said, wanting Fred to know that he was trying hard to see something.

She came to a stop, still wearing the rope. Fred walked to her shoulder, reached out and touched her. "Whoa there, little mama," he crooned. She flinched but then relaxed as Fred rubbed her neck.

"Those babies were all halter-broke when they were weaned. Ain't been handled since. Bring me that halter and rope hanging over there."

Ben climbed through the fence and handed him a rope

halter with a lead rope knotted to it. Fred tied the halter on her head and rubbed his hand all over the colt's face, neck, and around her ears.

"See, this little filly remembers," he said, picking up his lass rope. "You just take your time, keep 'em calm."

"Yeah, this is a little different than what my dad does," Ben commented. "He kind of jerks them around, shows them who's boss."

"His horses know he's boss alright. They're scared of him," Fred said. He removed the loop and neatly coiled up his lass rope. "I don't want my horses scared of me. I want them to trust me. I want them to be my pardner."

Pardner? Dad always calls me his pardner. I like being his pardner.

"Dad says a horse is just a tool," Ben said.

"Well, he's kind of right," Fred mused, rubbing the colt with the coils of his lass rope—her back, belly, legs, rump. "He's a buckaroo's most important tool, but if you treat him like a pardner, not a slave, he'll give you his all."

"I wouldn't want to be a slave," Ben said. He glanced at his watch, getting impatient. What about the other colts?

"You think we're just standing here wasting time? I'm letting old Roany learn that being with me is a good thing. But now I'm gonna ask her to go. Get back out of the way."

Ben climbed through the fence rails, embarrassed. Was Fred a mind reader or something?

Chapter 4

"Go on there, Sally," Fred said affectionately. Raising his coiled lass rope in his right hand, he fed out the halter rope with his left as the filly moved away. Ben couldn't believe how kindly Fred spoke to her. It seemed so unlike him.

"Is that her name—Sally?" Ben asked.

"Naw," Fred said with a laugh. "I call all the girls Sally." He watched the filly while talking to Ben.

"See how little I had to do to get her to move her feet? No need to smack her on the butt."

"My dad would have whacked her with the rope and yelled 'Git up!'"

The colt circled the pen.

"Come here, kid," Fred said, still watching the circling horse. Ben hopped off the fence and trotted toward him. When he stopped, Fred jabbed him in the ribs and yelled, "Now move over!"

Surprised and mad, Ben jumped away. Fred just laughed.

"Now come on back here, kid," Fred said, grinning. "Don't worry."

Uncertain, Ben approached.

Without touching him, Fred waved his hand in Ben's direction, saying kindly, "Now would you mind moving over a little?"

Confused, Ben stepped over, shaking his head. Fred turned from the horse, who had stopped, and looked straight at Ben for the first time.

"What did you just learn?"

Ben scowled, wondering what Fred meant.

"Well, I sure don't like it when you yell and poke me."

"And when I called you back, you didn't exactly come up to me like you trusted me." Fred chuckled.

"Well, I thought you might do it again," Ben said.

"Exactly!" Fred said excitedly.

"You didn't need to be so rude," Ben said. "You could have asked me a little nicer."

"Like I did the second time?"

"Yeah."

"So...what did you just learn about a horse?" Fred cocked his head, waiting.

A light came on inside Ben's head. He thought about his dad, about Fred, about the horse.

He said slowly, "So horses have feelings? Kind of like us?" He paused. "And if you're rude or scare them, they won't trust you?"

Fred grinned and gave a big nod. "You just taught yourself something real important!"

Ben took a big breath. *I can SEE it!* Fuzzy thoughts began to focus, as if he had turned the lens of his binoculars. He remembered how Black Bob jumped when he had kicked him, and how softly he moved when Ben asked him more politely.

Fred interrupted his thoughts. "Now pay attention. You're going to work the next one."

Ben felt nervous and relieved at the same time— relieved that he was finally going to get to do something, but nervous about trying to please Fred.

"Run another one in, kid."

Ben turned a little sorrel into the alley. Fred let it into the roundpen and let the roan out, and Ben turned her back into the pen with the others.

"Okay, kid, can you rope him?"

"I'll try."

He built a loop and started swinging it. The colt stood still, watching him curiously. Ben's loop flew through the air, landing on the colt's rump and sliding off. He trotted a few steps, then stopped, looking at Ben.

"Old Sorrelly's not as spooky as the roan," Fred commented.

Ben missed his second loop too. "Why don't we just wait till they're old enough and then saddle them and ride them, like my dad does?"

Fred watched as Ben coiled his rope again. "We're just handling them and getting them ready. They'll be easier to start."

"My dad wants them to buck. He says that's the fun part! He wants me to buck them out."

"I'd just as soon leave the buck *in* them. When he gets as old as me, he'll figure that out too."

On the third try, Ben snagged him. The colt jumped back, slung his head a little as he felt the pressure of the rope around his neck, and then stood.

"Good. Walk up and rub on him," Fred said.

Ben noticed the small compliment. He coiled up his slack and approached the colt's head with his hand extended. Eyes big and nostrils flared, the colt backed away.

"Don't come straight at his face like that. A spooky colt might strike at you—how do you think I got that scar between my eyes? Come in at an angle, to his shoulder."

Ben circled around. The colt stood uncertainly as he touched him on the withers.

"Watch his hind foot—he's got it cocked. Watch his eye—that'll tell you if he's thinking about kicking."

Too many things to think about!

"Rub on him. His head...his neck...see how far back you can get. Watch those hind feet."

Not standing too close, Ben cautiously rubbed the colt's hip, his eyes glued to that hind foot.

He felt a bump against his back.

"Watch it—he's about to taste you!" Fred yelled. "Quit acting so sneaky. You're making him nervous."

"What do you mean—sneaky?" Ben protested, turning to Fred. "You just said he might kick and he might bite!"

Fred strode over to the colt and took the rope. "Look. You touch him, you rub him, you watch his feet, you watch his teeth, you watch his eye, you've got to notice everything!"

While he talked, he moved around the colt, rubbing him everywhere. "But you've got to act confident so he'll be confident in you. Like this. On both sides."

The colt relaxed under Fred's expert handling. His head dropped lower and he gave a little sigh.

"So how did you get that scar between your eyes?"

Fred rubbed his forehead. "Well, I knew this colt might strike, but I got careless and got in his face. He pawed me right between the eyes and broke my nose."

Ben cringed. "Ooooh!"

"All I could think about was the brand new chaps I had on. I bent over and walked backwards to keep the wind from blowing that blood all over my chaps."

They both laughed. Fred handed Ben the halter and rope. "Here, put this on and move him around a little."

He coached Ben a bit more and helped him with the other colts. After a lunch break, they worked the rest of the afternoon.

Fred nodded as he turned the last one out. "Yep, I think you're starting to see. Each one is different. They tell you what they're thinking, and what they're about to do, if you've got eyes to *see*."

Ben said slowly, "It almost feels like I'm learning to speak another language."

"Exactly. You're starting to read their body language, and they're reading yours."

"I can kind of understand what they're saying now. But it's harder to get them to understand me."

"You'll get better at it."

"I think I see now why you didn't want me to start with Soapsuds today," Ben said. "At first I was mad this morning, but now I'm glad you showed me some stuff I need to know. I sure don't want to mess him up."

"I know you were mad, kid." Fred grinned. "But there's a lot more to it than you think. You've got to learn patience around horses."

A scowl of disbelief crossed Ben's face. *Fred? Patient? What a laugh!*

"I know what you're thinking," Fred said, cackling like a hen. "I ain't as patient with people as I am with horses."

Ben's cheeks burned. How could Fred know what he was thinking?

Fred laughed again. "Yep, I can read *your* body language just like I can read a horse. And your face tells me you're plumb tuckered out. Now get out of here."

Tired and hungry, Ben climbed onto his four-wheeler. His head was spinning with new ideas—ideas he couldn't share with his dad.

But *when* would they start his colt? Fred hadn't said another word about Soapsuds.

Chapter 5

Sunday morning, Ben and his parents got up early enough to make the hour-long drive to Elko for church. As he and his dad shined their town boots before leaving, Ben admired his dad's rugged good looks. All cleaned up in his Sunday jeans and shirt, his dark hair neatly combed, Pete cut a handsome figure.

Reaching for his hat, Ben swelled his chest as big as he could, trying to look like his dad. He cleared his throat and said in his lowest, most manly voice, "I'm ready to go, Dad."

"How do I look?" Susie asked, primping in front of the mirror.

"Great," Pete said, knotting a shiny blue wildrag around his neck, "but why are you wearing *that* dress? What if we break down? That's not too practical this time of year."

"Oh, you're always saying that, and we never do. I like this dress."

"That coat doesn't look too warm," Pete warned.

"But I like it with this outfit. We'll be in the pickup with the heater on." She grabbed her purse and a Bible.

Pete shrugged. "Whatever you say. Got your piano music?"

"No, it's not my Sunday to play."

"Okay, let's load up." Pete grabbed his thermos of coffee and they headed for the truck.

After Ben's mom slid to the middle, he climbed in and sat by the door. They headed down the three-mile driveway to the paved road. Ben got out and opened and closed both the wire gates, making sure no cows got through behind them. He knew the rules about gates: Closed gates must be left closed. Open gates must be left open. Whoever sits on the passenger side mans the gates.

His dad always said, "The smart cowboy sits in the middle." When Ben was little, he sat in the middle and his mom opened the gates. Now Ben was too old to sit in the middle. He let his mom and dad sit side by side, and he handled the gates.

When they hit pavement, they turned toward Elko. The other direction would take them to their own little town of Greeley. Greeley didn't have a church, only a two-room school, a tiny post office, a small bar and store combo, and a community hall.

As they picked up speed along the empty valley road, Pete said, "Pour me a shot of coffee, would you, dear?"

Susie reached under the seat for the thermos and slowly poured a little steaming liquid into the thermos cup. Careful not to spill any on her dress, she handed it to Pete.

They drove down the valley, passing few houses and

endless waves of dusty gray-green sagebrush. Here and there, cattle grazed on alfalfa stubble left from the last cutting of hay.

Horse Canyon loomed above the Circle A ranch. In spring and summer, melting snow drained down toward the ranch, forming Horse Creek (pronounced "crick" rather than "creek," as Ben always informed their city visitors).

Other ranches nestled along the base of the majestic Ruby Mountains, which rose abruptly from the high-desert valley floor. Each ranch, marked by a cluster of cottonwood trees, sat below the mouth of a small canyon, where yearly snowmelt formed spring runoff that watered their fields and meadows.

"What's up ahead?" Susie asked, pointing out the window in front of them.

"Looks like Leroy stopped on the side of the road," Pete said, slowing. "Better see if he needs help."

Susie checked her watch. "Just make sure we're not late."

A dented flatbed pickup pulling a rusty gooseneck trailer sat on the left side of the road near an old yellowed haystack. Pete pulled up and stopped beside it, in the middle of the empty road, rolling down his window and turning off the motor.

"Hey, Leroy. You broke down or something?"

Leroy rolled his window down too. He didn't look up as he cranked on the starter.

"She just quit on me. I'm headed down to my other

place to check on some cows." He shook his head and scowled as the starter growled slower and slower. "This pickup's a piece of junk," he said with disgust.

"Better not run down the battery," Pete warned, getting out. "Here, pop that hood. Ben, get me a rag."

Leroy got out and joined Pete in front of his truck. Ben, rummaging behind the seat, found a grease rag. Using the rag, Pete unscrewed the air filter and lifted it off. He peered underneath and sniffed.

"She doesn't appear to be flooded." He screwed the air filter back in place.

"It's not the fuel filter," Leroy said. "I just changed that a week ago."

As the three of them leaned on the front of the old pickup, Ben shivered. Nevada was usually windy like this, and the fall morning was nippy.

Pete nodded toward the trailer. "Isn't that the mare you showed in Elko at the Labor Day fair?"

"Yep," Leroy said. "She sure did nice for me. If that young whipper-snapper Seth hadn't been showing that gelding of his, we would have won the stockhorse class."

"Yeah, he's a pretty fair hand. I know Fred sure likes the way he handles a horse."

Ben looked over at his mother. He knew she'd be checking her watch, getting mad at Pete for shooting the breeze when they were supposed to be going somewhere. He nudged his dad, hinting.

Pete rubbed his finger on a big dark spot on the fender. "What's that? Looks like powder burns."

Leroy laughed. "Yeah, from shooting ground squirrels. Man, that's a sorry-looking haystack," he said, shaking his head.

"Yeah, it's so old, I sure wouldn't feed that junk to *our* cows. I wonder what Alphonso is planning to do with it?"

Leroy laughed. "He ought to just burn it down!"

Pete laughed too. "Hey Ben, grab me that can of starting fluid, would you?"

"Sure, Dad."

Finally, thought Ben. He climbed into the bed of the truck and opened his dad's big toolbox. He sorted through the parts and cans mixed in with the tools—carburetor cleaner, WD-40, a quart of oil, a funnel...and the can of starting fluid he was looking for. He slammed the lid down, jumped over the side of the bed, and handed his dad the can.

"Good thing you came along, neighbor!" Leroy said cheerfully as he climbed back into the cab. "I might have been setting here quite a while."

Pete squirted a little starting fluid in the carburetor. "Okay," he hollered. "Fire that bugger up!"

Leroy cranked on the starter.

BOOM. The truck backfired but didn't start.

Ben jumped back in surprise. He wrinkled his nose and laughed. "Sheesh, that smelled like fire!"

His laugh turned into a yell. "Dad! It *is* a fire!"

Chapter 6

Flames crackled in the weeds on the ditch bank near the exhaust pipe.

"Oh, cripes!" Pete raced around the truck as Leroy leaped out and slammed the door behind him. Pete unzipped his jacket and jerked it off. Leroy unbuckled his chaps, kicked them off, and swung them over his head by the belt. They beat at the flames gathering speed in the wind. *Slap! Slap! Slap!*

From the open pickup window, Ben's mom yelled, "Pete! That's your best jacket!"

Ben froze for a moment, looking frantically from his dad to his mom—then to the trailer, where the horse was dancing around and whinnying nervously. He ran to the back of the trailer and unlatched the tailgate. As he untied the lead rope, he crooned to the snorting horse, "Whoa there, easy girl, easy there."

Susie scooted over to the driver's side and started the pickup, parking it farther down the road on the other side.

Pete yelled to her, "Take the horse!" She jumped out of the truck, clutching her light coat around her. Clicking in her high heels, she hurried to meet Ben as he led the spooked mare out of the trailer.

He handed her the rope. "Take her across the road and hold her, Mom!"

Click, click, clop, clop. She led the mare to the far ditch bank and let it graze as she shivered in the wind, her hair whipping in her face.

"Get the shovel!" Pete yelled. The flames, blowing toward the stackyard, crackled and crept ahead of the men.

Ben ran back to the truck and reached over the side for the shovel that they always packed with them. He raced toward the men.

Adrenaline pumped fiercely through his tense body as he began scooping dirt and dropping it on the flames. At home, his dad had taught him to smother flames with dirt when their burn barrel showered sparks into the weeds. If the flames didn't get into the sagebrush, it worked great.

Ben's face glowed from the pressing heat. Fear and excitement filling him with strength, he pushed the shovel blade along the top of the ground. With a quick toss, he flipped the scoop of dirt forward onto the dancing flames. Scoop, toss, scoop, toss—working rhythmically, keeping one eye on the nearby haystack. The frazzled dry edges of the old yellow bales could easily catch a spark in the wind.

With the three of them working, they began to gain on the fire. Just as they reached the barb wire fence of the stackyard, the wind changed direction. The flames now blew back toward the burnt ground, where no more fuel remained. All three straightened up, panting and wiping their sweaty foreheads.

"Whew!" Leroy said, his chest heaving. "I'm about out of puff!"

Pete slapped Ben on the back. "Good work, Ben."

Eyes watering from the acrid-smelling smoke, Ben leaned on the shovel, trying to catch his breath. "Wow, that was close!" he gasped.

The shifting wind caught a smoldering tumbleweed. It somersaulted through the fence toward the haystack and hit a fallen bale lying by itself.

The dry hay instantly ignited. As the bale turned into a fireball, the wind blew the sparks into the old haystack. Whoosh! In seconds, flames engulfed the entire stack.

Pete, Leroy, and Ben sprinted toward the haystack, but the intense heat drove them back.

"Susie, get in the truck! Go for help!" Pete yelled. "Ben, go take the horse."

Leaving his shovel, Ben ran to his mom. She hurried toward him, tugging on the horse's lead rope. In her haste, she tripped on her high heels and almost fell.

"You okay, mom?" Ben grabbed her elbow.

"Darn it! I twisted my ankle bad. I hope it's not sprained." She groaned. "I don't know if I can drive—you'd better go, Ben. I'll just hold the horse."

Ben hesitated, then raced to the truck and jumped in. It started right up, and he jammed it into gear, kicking up gravel as he took off. He glanced at his mom, hoping she would be okay with the horse. She looked worried.

He pressed the gas pedal hard, smoothly clutching and shifting as he accelerated. It was several miles to the nearest house.

Dear God, please let someone be home! Please take care of my mom and dad!

His dad had taught him to drive several years ago. But driving around the ranch is not like driving fast down the pavement when your heart is pounding, your chest is heaving, your knees are shaking, and sweat is pouring off you. He licked the salty dust off his lips.

Ben had never driven this fast. Strangely, he had never felt so alive in all his life.

Thank you that there's no one on the road. And, dear God, please make the wind stop!

Ben kept checking the rear view mirror. The inferno looked huge. If it spread into the sagebrush, they could have a major fire on their hands.

Why, oh why, doesn't Greeley have a fire truck yet? Panic flared through his chest at the thought of wildfire.

Slowing down, Ben pulled into the gravel road leading into his buddy Derek's place. He had often driven to Derek's the back way, but never on the pavement. His parents only let him drive on the dirt roads out through the ranches and sagebrush.

Ben veered to the side as Derek's dad came roaring down the lane and passed him. Derek, standing in the yard, waved his arms wildly as Ben approached.

"We saw the fire from the kitchen window!" Derek said, jerking the passenger door open and jumping in. "We got the binoculars and saw you guys down there! Mom's calling everybody. Dad took shovels. He said for us to bring wet saddle blankets and gunny sacks. Drive to the barn, quick!"

At the barn, they found as many sacks and blankets as they could and threw them in the closest water trough and then into the back of the truck. Ben gunned the truck back down the drive and out onto the pavement. Ahead, the black smoke now billowed straight up.

The wind must have stopped. Thank you, Lord!

A few other pickups lined the road and men with shovels converged on the scene. At the sight of smoke, people in the valley dropped what they were doing and came to help. Ben recognized one of the ranch trucks— some of the Circle A cowboys must have shown up. Several men unloaded a tractor and disc from a flatbed trailer.

After Ben parked the truck, he and Derek hauled the dripping sacks and heavy blankets out to the men. The shrinking haystack crackled and snapped, but not a whisper of wind remained.

Although the intense heat held them back, the men encircled the fire, throwing shovelfuls of dirt as the tractor began to disc a firebreak around the stackyard. Several men swung the wet sacks and blankets at smoldering embers or slapped them at flames.

Ben noticed that someone else was holding the horse. He scanned the vehicles until he spotted his mom sitting in a pickup with another woman. He wandered over toward his dad, listening to the conversations.

"Did you notice how that wind just quit? What luck!"

"Yeah, if that wind had kept up, this fire would be

halfway to my place by now."

"Man, I just happened to look over this way and see that smoke."

"I was out in the shop. My wife took the call. I saw her standing on the step, yelling and waving like crazy. I came running!"

"We need that fire truck. What's the holdup anyhow? We ordered it months ago."

Pete spoke up. "I'll call Elko tomorrow. Ben and I volunteer to bring it home as soon as it arrives. What do you say, Ben?"

"Can we really, Dad?" Ben's voice cracked.

"Well, I'd say you earned it today."

"You're darn right he did," Leroy said. "I dare say that boy's got the makings of a fire fighter." Derek joined them. "Thanks go to both you boys!"

"Well, we're gonna find out how tough he is pretty soon," Pete said, winking at Ben. "I got a couple of colts I want him to buck out."

"Cool!" Derek said. "I'll come and watch. I want to see him get maaaaaashed!" He punched Ben playfully, then ducked as Ben punched him back, grinning.

By now, only charred black ground and glowing red embers remained where the fast-burning haystack once stood. As the heat slacked off, the circle of men tightened, putting out the last embers.

"Ben, you and Mom might as well go home. I'll stay and ride home with the Circle A crew. No need for you to hang around."

Ben nodded. "See you at school tomorrow," he called as Derek left to join his dad.

He kicked at dirt clods as he headed for the pickup.

He still doesn't think I'm tough enough. "Buck out some colts." Great—and now Derek is going to watch!

He shuddered as he pictured his head getting maaaaaashed.

Chapter 7

As the pickup neared the barn, Ben spotted Fred in the corral. *What? Is he catching Soapsuds?*

"Mom, stop! Let me out!"

His mom stopped the truck, and Ben jumped out and ran to the fence.

Fred waved him over. "You coming or ain't you?" he yelled, grouchy as ever.

"I'll be right back!" Ben yelled, racing to the truck and scrambling in. "Hurry, Mom! I've got to get back here quick!"

She frowned. "You didn't say anything about helping Fred today. And why wasn't he at the fire?"

"I don't know!" Ben said breathlessly, wondering why Fred hadn't told him his plans.

At the house, he changed quickly, leaving his church clothes lying helter-skelter on the floor. Not waiting for lunch, he wolfed down a banana and gulped a glass of milk. Wiping his milk mustache, he stuffed two cookies into his mouth, yelled, "Bye, Mom," and flew out the door. He jumped on the four-wheeler, revved the motor, and spun the wheels as he took off.

"Turn that gray colt into the roundpen," Fred barked as Ben shut off the motor. "I'll catch that yellow horse. We might need him a little later."

Ben nodded. He grabbed the halter and rope from the tack room. Ducking under the corral fence, he trotted across the dusty pen.

Half smiling, he recalled that fateful day at the corral last summer with the crazy ground squirrel, the orange slipknot, and the runaway horses. The movie picture played in his head every time he passed this corral. But... that day was the reason Soapsuds no longer belonged to him.

"Hey, Soapsuds," he crooned, rubbing the warm, gray neck. The colt's velvety white ears flicked back and forth.

"You hoping I'll brush you?" Ben slipped a halter on his head. After Pete halter-broke the colt as a weanling, he forbid Ben to fool with him—he said horses weren't pets. But Ben had often brushed Soapsuds as he munched his hay. With all his heart, Ben had been waiting for this day.

He could have just run the colt into the alley, but haltering him gave Ben a chance to handle him. Leading him through the gate, he turned him into the roundpen and removed the halter and lead, hanging them on a fence post.

As Fred tied his saddled horse at the tie rack by the barn, he yelled, "Grab your saddle and snaffle."

Saddles on racks lined the tack room wall. Above them, bridles hung from large nails, or coffee cans with their bottoms nailed to the wall. Spade bits—with silver conchos on the headstalls and braided rawhide reins. Hackamores—with smooth braided rawhide bosals and prickly horsehair reins. Snaffles—with jointed mouthpieces and rope McCarty's, like Ben would use to start the colt.

He found his snaffle, sliding the headstall and rope reins into the crook of his left elbow. His left hand pulled the blanket off the top of his saddle. With his right hand, he jerked his stock saddle off the rack and onto his hip. Leaning heavily to the left, he stumped out to the pen— stirrups bumping his ankles—and dumped everything on the ground by the fence.

Fred joined him, carrying a coiled lass rope and a rope halter with a long lead rope. He let himself into the roundpen, dropping the halter in the middle of it.

"Come here, kid." He handed Ben the lass rope. "Here, use this to move him around a little."

Ben shook the coiled rope toward the colt. He moved off around the corral to the left at a stiff trot.

"We'll work him a little, then rope him."

Ben's eyes followed the gray colt around the pen, drinking in the sight of him. He pictured himself on the colt's back, riding out through the sagebrush, gathering a herd of white-faced cattle...

"See that attitude?"

Fred's voice jerked Ben back to reality. He studied the colt. "What attitude?"

"See that kink in his tail? See that high head and clamped jaw—those tight lips, flared nostrils, big eyes?

All that tells me about his attitude. He's tight and worried."

Ben concentrated. Why couldn't he see what Fred saw?

A pickup rumbled down the long, bumpy driveway. They both turned to look as Pete, Seth, and Reggie drove up and stopped.

"Hey, Fred, you missed all the excitement," Pete said as he got out. "Leroy and I lit Alphonso's haystack on fire. We had half the valley down there putting it out."

"Yeah, well, I slept in. I was puking last night," Fred said. "I heard the phone but didn't answer it." He looked at Ben apologetically. "Then I forgot you'd be off to Elko this morning."

Ben shrugged his shoulders. "It's okay."

Seth and Reggie sauntered over to the roundpen, pretending to puke and making gross noises. "Mind if we watch?"

Fred grunted. "Suit yourself."

"How's that colt doing?" Seth asked. Ben shrugged his shoulders. Seth, barely out of high school, was Ben's best friend on the ranch, and treated him almost like a little brother. He and the other unmarried cowboys lived in the bunkhouse.

"Looks like we got here just in time to see the show," Reggie said with a grin. Tall and lanky, he carried a can of beer.

Pete joined them.

"Well, slap that saddle on him and buck him out!"

Ben looked uncertainly from Pete to Fred. "Fred said

it's important to get his attitude right so he trusts us."

Pete snorted. "When I was your age, I had bucked out lots of horses!"

Ben chewed his lip. *Why did he have to say that in front of everybody?*

He hoped Fred would say something to his dad. Fred just spit in the dirt. But when Ben looked at Soapsuds, he remembered how the black horse felt—like riding a cloud. That's what he wanted, no matter what his dad thought or said.

Leaning forward, Pete spread his elbows on the fence and hooked a boot heel on the bottom rail. "Look at him hold that head up high, look at him wave that tail and prance, look at those big eyes. He's sure got a high-spirited, flashy way of moving." Pete grinned proudly.

Ben frowned. *How can Dad and Fred look at that colt and see completely different attitudes? They don't SEE the same things.*

Fred glanced at Pete and then said to Ben, "Now turn him a couple of times each way. Direct those feet."

Ben moved around the pen, using the coiled rope to turn the colt and move him out.

"Let's see you rope him. We want him to learn to accept the rope."

"Yeah, now we're going to see some action!" Reggie said.

Ben shook out his coils and built a loop. As he swung the big loop over his head, Soapsuds moved nervously away from the humming rope. With a flick of his wrist, Ben let the loop fly. It settled over the colt's haunches, dragging on the ground. Soapsuds squirted forward in surprise.

"Let him wear it," Fred said. "Just let him get used to it."

Ben admired the colt's powerful movements. His rhythmic strides had a hypnotic effect on Ben. He felt like he was in a trance. Even Fred's voice took on a dream-like sound.

"Can you drop a loop over his head?"

"Huh?" Ben snapped back to attention. "I'll try."

As Soapsuds trotted around the pen, Ben jerked his rope back in, quickly coiled it, and built another loop, turning and watching the colt as he swung it over his head. Letting the loop fly, he forgot to open his left hand and feed out the coils. The loop fell short.

"Take your time, kid. Try again."

Ben took a deep breath, knowing everyone was watching. The second loop settled over the colt's head. Ben sucked in his breath with pride.

"Atta boy," Pete said approvingly. "Jerk him around now. Show him who's boss."

Ignoring Pete, Fred said, "Just let him feel that rope tighten until he comes to a stop."

Ben looked from Fred to Pete. Who should he listen to? As Soapsuds gave to the rope, slowed and stopped, Ben gave him slack. He could see the trust and curiosity in the colt's big soft eyes.

I guess I'll just listen to Soapsuds.

Chapter 8

As Ben rubbed his coils all over the colt's body, Pete retrieved his thermos from the pickup, returned to the corral, and poured himself a cup of coffee. "Look at those muscular hindquarters," he said. "He's a stout bugger. I'll bet he can buck like a son-of-a-gun!"

Fred shook his head. "My bronc-riding days are over. That's why I've got Ben here to get on him first!"

"Yeah!" Pete hollered. "Bring it on, Ben!"

A jolt of fear shot through Ben's stomach. Would Soapsuds really buck with him? Would he throw him in the dirt head first? Would his head get *maaaaaashed*? What would that feel like? Would he cry and act like a baby in front of everyone? He swallowed hard.

Why does Dad only care about bucking? His fear shifted briefly to anger. *And Fred doesn't really care about teaching me! He's just using me so HE doesn't get bucked off.*

Hauling in the saddle and blanket, Fred sent Ben out. He haltered the colt and removed the lass rope, and then approached him, the blanket in his right hand, rope in his left. Eyes big, the colt skittered away from it. Reggie and Seth hooted with glee.

Fred calmly followed the colt around until he stood still, rolling his eyes as the blanket touched him. Fred rubbed the blanket all over—under his belly, down his legs, around his neck, over his rump, and flicked it on and off his back several times.

Soapsuds flinched but stood his ground. Fred stepped to the other side and did the same things. Soon the colt stood quietly, no longer alarmed.

Pete sighed loudly. "Well, I'm getting bored," he said sarcastically. "If you're not going to put on a show for us, I've got some stuff to clean up in the tack room." He turned and headed for the barn.

Anger flooded Ben. *He only wants to watch if I might get bucked off! He doesn't care if I'm learning to be a good horseman.*

Fred scratched the colt's withers. "He's a sensible colt."

"Sensible, huh?" Reggie snorted. "We'll see how sensible he acts when someone gets on him!"

Ben's stomach tightened again. Now he wasn't so sure he wanted to ride the colt.

Fred centered the blanket on the colt's back, the rope draped over his left arm. Hoisting the saddle, he let it down gently onto the blanket. The scrawny little old man handled the heavy stock saddle as easily as if it were made out of paper maché. He cinched it up carefully but quickly.

"Now, about this saddle," he explained as he worked. "Some horses figure out right away that it won't hurt them, and they just ignore it. Some get in a big dither and go to bucking. And that's fine—they get their bucking over with before you ever get on 'em."

He removed the halter and backed away from the colt. "Okay, here we go!"

Ben peered over the fence, holding his breath.

For a few seconds, Soapsuds stood humped up like a camel and then walked off stiff-legged. Four...slow...steps. Then all hell broke loose.

The colt exploded. He sprang forward, slinging his head toward the ground and shooting his hind feet high into the air, squealing like a pig. The stirrups slapped up and down against his ribs, egging him on, and the lass rope tied to the right side clattered against the saddle.

Ben grabbed the rail of the fence, his heart pounding. "Ho-ly cry-in' out loud," he whispered slowly.

"Yee-haw!" Reggie yelled, swinging his hat over his head. "Let 'er rip!" He fanned his hat, laughing, as the colt bucked past him.

Soapsuds came apart in mid-air, all four feet high off the ground. Grunting, he twisted his belly toward the sky— the saddle horn sideways, then on top again. Landing on all fours, he reared, walking on his hind feet, shaking his head and striking the air with his front feet.

And just like that, it was over.

Seth took off his hat and scratched his head. Slowly he breathed, "Hell-fire and dang-na-tion!"

"What a woss-hoffer!" exclaimed Reggie in admiration.

The colt stood, blowing hard. The wild look left his eyes, and he stared curiously at Fred. Ben spied Pete standing in the doorway of the tack room, watching.

Fred shook the coils of his lass rope. The colt trotted off as calmly as if he'd been born with a saddle on his back. He smartly circled the roundpen, ears pointed forward.

"Now, ain't that the danged-est thing you ever seen?" Fred shook his head. "He plumb blows his plug, and now he's all business."

Fred walked up to the colt and rubbed his face. Lowering his head, Soapsuds noisily blew air out his nostrils.

"Well, kid," Fred said, "there's nothing left to do but get on him. You ready?"

"Show 'em what you got, Ben," hollered Pete, grinning.

Ben shivered, partly in anticipation, partly in dread. Just get on and buck him out, his dad had said. *Yeah, right,* Ben thought. *I wonder how many broken bones I'll have tonight? I'll probably be spending the night in the hospital.*

Stalling for time, Ben asked nervously, "So you want me to get on him now?" His voice cracked.

Reggie snickered, but Seth jabbed an elbow in his side, whispering, "Shut up."

Then to Ben, he joked, "Cowboy up! Show us your stuff!"

Ben tried to smile and raised his eyebrows uncertainly.

"Only one of two things can happen," Seth said. "He'll either muck you out, or he won't."

Ben caught the twinkle in his eye and gave a shaky laugh.

"I don't know if I can stay on him," he admitted,

hesitating with one foot on the fence rail.

Fred laughed. "Just relax, sit deep, grab your Cheyenne roll with one hand and your lass rope with the other!"

Ben climbed slowly onto the top rail and straddled it.

"He's as ready as he'll ever be," Fred said. "Like as not, he won't buck. He's already accepted the rope, the blanket, the saddle. I don't think he'll have any trouble accepting you. That's the whole point of everything we just did."

"Go on," Reggie urged, slapping him on the back.

Ben took a deep breath. Grinning self-consciously, he hopped down. "Well, let's get on with it, if I'm ever going to learn to be a buckaroo."

One corner of Fred's mouth turned up in a half-smile. "Hand me the snaffle," he called to Seth. "And fetch me that yellow horse, Reggie."

As Ben approached the colt, Fred took the bridle from Seth and said, "Don't worry, kid. I got a plan."

Fred slipped the reins over the colt's head, eased the bit into his mouth, and slid the headstall gently over his ears. He buckled the throatlatch and draped the reins over the saddle horn.

"Here, kid," he said, handing Ben the McCarty. Ben took the leading end of the rope reins.

Reggie opened the gate and led the yellow horse to Fred. Still holding his coiled lass rope, Fred stepped into his saddle and quickly built a loop, tossing it so it landed in front of the colt's hind feet.

"Lead him forward a step," he said to Ben. When Soapsuds stepped one foot into the loop, Fred pulled up his slack. He took a turn around his horn, holding his reins and coils with his left hand. With his right hand on the rope so he could slip his dally if needed, he backed his horse a few steps until the hind foot just lifted off the ground.

Pete snorted, shook his head, and disappeared into the tack room again. Ben bit his lip. *Isn't he going to watch?*

"Always tuck that McCarty under your belt," Fred directed. "I don't expect we'll have any trouble, but it's a good habit to make—if he bucks you off, you've still got a hold of him. And tighten your rope strap before you get on."

Ben stepped to the colt's right side, reached up toward the big horn and reefed on the strap around his lass rope, snugging it up good and rebuckling it. As he returned to the left side, he pulled his black felt hat down tighter on his head like he'd seen his dad do.

"Okay, kid, step aboard."

Chapter 9

Ben took the reins and a handful of mane in his left hand. Holding the big wooden stirrup with his right hand, he hesitated, hoping his fear didn't show.

"Get on," Fred snapped impatiently. "He can't do anything while I've got his foot."

Ben gingerly put his left foot in the stirrup. Taking a deep breath, he grabbed the saddle with his right hand and pulled himself up. He swung his right leg smoothly over the colt's rump, careful not to poke him with his boot.

Gently lowering himself into the saddle, he picked up his right stirrup with the toe of his boot and tucked the doubled-up end of the McCarty into his belt. His heart pounded, his hands shook. The bucking scene ran through his mind like an instant replay.

"Rub his neck," Fred directed. "There, he looks pretty relaxed. Now grab your rope and your Cheyenne roll. Leave your rein over the horn. If he wads up, I'll stop his feet."

With his left hand behind him on the cantle, Ben got a hold of the lass rope strapped snugly to the right side of the horn.

"If he bucks, just relax, keep your elbows in and your chin down."

Clucking, Fred loosened the rope, giving Soapsuds his foot. The colt moved off hesitantly, trailing the rope behind him.

"Let go now and then," Fred called, "to rub his neck and his rump."

After circling the corral, Fred stopped his horse, tightening up the rope so the colt had to stop and give his foot.

"Now this time, you tell him to move."

Blowing out through his mouth, Ben tried to relax. He gently flapped his legs on the colt's sides. Soapsuds didn't feel the least bit tense as they moved off.

"Now pick up one rein a little to stop him," Fred called.

The colt gave his head to the side, slowed, and stopped. Fred shook the slack in his rope until it fell from the colt's foot.

"He's fine. You don't need this."

"Are you sure?" asked Ben nervously. He felt safer with that rope on the foot...just in case.

"Let me move him around," Fred said. "You just sit there."

Fred swung his rope until the colt walked off and then sped up. Soapsuds felt strong as he trotted out.

"Don't tighten up—give him slack. He can't run off in this corral. Now pick up your right rein and look to the right—get him to follow your body. That's it. Now the other way."

Ben loosened his reins and sat deeper in the saddle, letting his body move with the colt. Riding Soapsuds felt great.

"There you go," Fred yelled approvingly. "Now you're starting to go with him." He sat in the middle on his horse, watching them trot around him.

"Now pick up one rein until he walks." The colt slowed and Ben gave him slack again. "You're handling your reins better. That was good timing with your slack."

Ben relaxed enough to grin at Fred.

"They're looking pretty good," Seth observed.

"Dang! I thought we were gonna get another wild west show," Reggie complained.

"Let's tip him up into a lope," Fred said.

As the colt trotted faster, Ben felt him start to hump up.

"He's wadding up," warned Fred. "Turn him! Give him something else to think about. There you go! Now ask him again—I'll help you."

Fred swung his rope until Soapsuds broke into a lope. Ben delighted in his smooth, strong stride. How many times he had dreamed of this day. A momentary pang smote him as he reminded himself that Soapsuds wasn't really his.

He glimpsed his dad watching from the tackroom door, arms crossed over his chest. *Is he proud of me? Or...is he disappointed?*

"Now slow your body down, kid. Just quit riding. See what he does."

The colt dropped to a trot, then a walk.

Ben laughed. "It's magic! I didn't even use my reins."

"Pick up one rein and take him around the other way a bit." Fred moved him up again into a big trot, then a lope. Loping the powerful colt with his reins swinging loose made Ben feel like he owned the world.

"That's enough for today," Fred called after they'd circled the roundpen a few times. "Let's quit while we're ahead."

Ben didn't want to ever get off, but he brought the colt to a stop. He rubbed his neck and stroked his mane. "Good boy," he murmured. Reluctantly, he gathered his reins and a handful of mane in his left hand, and with his right hand on the horn, he started to get off.

"Wait," Fred called. "Remember, you're on a green colt. You only want your toes in the stirrups, so you don't get hung up if he scatters when you're halfway off. Let that toe slip out of the stirrup as quick as you can."

Ben wiggled the toes of his boots in the stirrups, trying to remember everything Fred had said. He swung out of the saddle smoothly and quickly.

When he hit the ground, his left foot slipped easily from the stirrup, and he rubbed the colt's neck, murmuring, "Hey, boy, thanks for not bucking me off."

As he helped Fred unsaddle the colt in the roundpen, Fred asked, "How about if you show up tomorrow after school for the next go-round?"

"Sure," Ben answered with enthusiasm. After he put Soapsuds away, he and Seth did chores, and then found

Pete in the tack room.

"Did you see me ride him, Dad?" Ben asked.

"Yeah, I poked my head out the door."

"What did you think? Wasn't he great?"

"He didn't even try you." Pete sounded disappointed. "I thought he'd show a little more fight than that."

Puzzled, Ben wondered, *Is he proud of me or not? Why does he want him to fight?*

Picking up a rag, Seth started greasing a set of leather reins. "Well, he sure came unglued with that saddle. But Fred took good care of Ben."

Pete snorted. "A broken bone or two ain't the end of the world. I've had a few of them myself."

"Well, there's plenty of time yet for bronc riding," Seth added. "He's still just a kid."

Just a kid! Ben practically choked. *I thought Seth was my friend!* He stomped off toward his four-wheeler.

"Hey, where are you going?" Pete called.

"Home," yelled Ben angrily without turning around.

Ben heard his dad ask Seth, "Now what the heck is his problem?"

Ben revved his motor and skidded his tires, cranking the handlebars hard.

Everyone treats me like a kid! Everyone except Fred.

Chapter 10

Riding home, Ben wished he could talk to his dad about Soapsuds and Fred, but how could he when his dad didn't seem to want to listen? Resentment piled up inside him like black storm clouds.

He doesn't want to know what I think or how I feel. Does he even care about my life?

His mother greeted him as he came in. "There's a good program on TV."

"I have homework," he said, "some reading to do before tomorrow." He closed his bedroom door behind him and only came out to do chores before dinner.

At the table, Susie said, "Well, how did your first ride go on Soapsuds?"

"Fine," he said and kept eating. She sighed.

As they were finishing dessert, his dad finally said, "You know, I've started lots of colts. I could help you with that colt."

Ben glared at his dad. "You're sorry he didn't buck me off today, aren't you?" He added sarcastically, "I'll bet you're disappointed that I don't have any broken bones."

"Ben!" exclaimed his mother.

"Now what's got into you?" demanded Pete.

"I heard what you said to Seth. You hope I'll get bucked off and break my bones!"

"That's not what I said," retorted Pete. "What I said was, a few bumps and bruises don't hurt anyone."

Ben's head felt like a volcano about to explode. He had to get out of there.

He pushed his chair back and set his dishes on the counter. Grabbing his jacket off the coat rack, he slammed out the kitchen door.

Outside, he hesitated, hearing his parents' voices. Unable to make out any words, he crept closer to the window.

His mom was saying, "So if that's not what you said, where did he get this idea about broken bones?"

"I was kidding. He takes things too seriously," answered Pete.

"Your idea of kidding can be a little harsh sometimes."

"Well, he could use a little toughening up."

Ben's blood boiled. He was so mad at his dad, he didn't care that eavesdropping was wrong. He kept listening.

"What's he going to do when some day he's way out in the sagebrush all by himself, and he bucks off and breaks something? You grit your teeth and get back on."

Ben chewed his lip, trying to imagine his dad getting on a horse with a broken bone. He shuddered, remembering his broken arm, years ago, and how the least movement hurt, even the jiggling of the pickup while they drove to Elko to the doctor.

Did that really happen to Dad? Or was he just making up a "what-if"?

He rode his four-wheeler down the road. Between the moonlight and his headlight, he could see Whitey and Bones eating. They looked up and nickered as he stopped and watched them for a while, wishing Soapsuds was still in that pasture with them.

I'd better not let on that I heard any of that, he thought as he rode home. *Dad would really chew on me for eavesdropping.*

Now he began to feel guilty. After all, how would he feel if his parents did that by *his* window when one of his friends was over?

Ben found that his four-wheeler seemed to be heading toward the barn, like it had a mind of its own. Toward Soapsuds. Yes, visiting Soapsuds would make him feel better. He parked by the corrals and turned off the motor.

There stood the colt, the moonlight casting a spell as it shone on his gray and white coat. Ben climbed up the fence and sat on the top rail. His heart did flip-flops as he relived their first ride.

Soapsuds lifted his head from the hay. Facing Ben, ears pricked forward, he gave a soft nicker. Ben's heart ached for the loss of his colt—his most prized possession. He had dreamed of the day he would be cowboying on his colt—the colt he had raised himself. Being a buckaroo, having his own ranch, running cattle in these mountains...

He sighed. Now Soapsuds belonged to Fred. He would soon be assigned to some buckaroo's string, to replace the horse that had died—all because of Ben's prank last summer.

Ben squeezed his eyes shut for a minute and then dashed the tears from his cheeks. When he looked up, there stood Soapsuds, right next to him. Ben reached out and touched him.

"Soapsuds," he whispered, stroking the colt. His dad had named him. He wasn't exactly a paint, a roan or a dapple-gray. Just the color of...soapsuds.

As his fingers scratched the colt's forehead and behind his ears, the colt moved closer, positioning himself for more scratches. His shoulder touched Ben's leg.

He's inviting me to slide right over onto his back!

Ben sucked in his breath and leaned over. His hands traveled down the colt's warm neck and grabbed handfuls of his thick gray-and-white-streaked mane. His heart beat faster.

Forgetting how the colt had bucked with the saddle, Ben only remembered the bliss of riding him. He wanted to feel that again. He wanted to ride him forever and ever, a never-ending ride.

Soapsuds nickered again, nuzzling Ben. That did it. Ben's right boot inched its way across the colt, who stood just close enough for Ben to slide on. He leaned farther off the fence rail.

His knee slid across the colt's back and his thigh. As he pushed off the fence with his other foot, Soapsuds snorted and stepped back. Ben lunged the rest of the way and clutched with his knees and heels.

The colt scooted forward and spun hard. Before Ben knew what happened, he landed on his butt with a thud. His dreams vanished as his thoughts came rudely back to earth. Struggling to his feet, he rubbed his hip and moaned.

Soapsuds moved uneasily around the pen, giving a few soft snorts. Ben approached him, his hand outstretched.

"Come here, boy. Whoa, boy. I'm sorry."

But Soapsuds wouldn't let him close. Ben tried to corner him, but the colt dashed away, showing Ben his heels in a pretend kick.

Ben's shoulders slumped, his face in a grimace. "Stupid, stupid me," he groaned, more miserable than when he drove up. He crawled through the fence, wincing in pain.

Alarmed, he realized he could not let anyone see him limping. No one must know he snuck a ride on Fred's colt.

He lifted his leg painfully over the seat of his four-wheeler, sat down and started the motor. To his guilty conscience, it sounded as loud as a jet engine in the still night air. Driving home, he worried that someone might have seen him.

When Ben walked in the house, his parents were in the living room, watching the news. He stopped and examined the cluster of photos on the kitchen wall. Rodeo and horse show pictures of his dad and his granddad—framed photographs and old yellowed newspaper clippings.

In one picture, he could just make out the cast on his dad's foot. A horse had fallen with him and broken his foot, and although it wasn't completely healed yet, Pete had insisted on showing this horse. He held the cast in the stirrup with big rubber bands.

"No doctor's going to tell me when I can ride and when I can't," he had told Ben. "And anyhow, we won that class." The silver platter sat on the bookshelf in the living room.

Was this what his dad had talked about? Or something else—something Ben didn't know about?

Maybe he did climb on a horse with a broken bone, mused Ben. The more he thought about it, the more it seemed like something his dad could do.

I'd sure like to ask him. But if I did, he'd know that I listened in on their argument.

From the sofa, his dad turned and looked over his shoulder at Ben standing in the kitchen. "What are you doing in there?" he asked.

"Oh, nothing," said Ben quickly, his heart skipping a beat. So many things to hide all of a sudden. Struggling not to limp, he gritted his teeth against the pain and disappeared down the hall into his room.

Chapter 11

Shortly after school on Monday, Ben met Fred at the barn. Black Bob stood saddled at the tie rack.

Fred barked orders. "Get that colt caught. Saddle him right here," he said.

Ben gritted his teeth as he forced himself not to limp in front of Fred.

"Okay," he said, grabbing a halter and lead rope. Fred sat on the barn porch on an upside-down bucket, watching.

After quickly brushing the colt, Ben centered the saddle blanket, fold to the front, and hoisted the heavy saddle into place. He lifted the front of the saddle and carefully pushed the fold of the blanket up into the fork, making an air pocket for the horse's withers.

Ben sweated from the pain as Fred's critical eyes followed him. *At least Fred doesn't know what happened.*

Fred grunted. "What's the matter, kid? You look like you just pooped a square turd."

Ben struggled to fake a smile. "Nothing's the matter," he lied.

He let down the cinch. Then he threaded the long leather latigo strap through the cinch ring several times, snugged it and buckled it, and tucked the end through the keeper. Soapsuds stood quietly as if he'd been saddled every day of his life.

Ben put his snaffle on the colt, straightened his forelock, and slid the rope reins over the colt's head, still holding the long end of the McCarty. He looked at Fred and cocked one eyebrow.

Fred nodded. "Take him to the roundpen," he said, getting up and heading for his horse. In the corral, Fred mounted the black while Ben closed the gate.

"Okay, get on him," he ordered.

Ben hesitated, replaying yesterday's events quickly in his mind. Fred didn't realize what all had happened. Things had changed.

"You think he'll buck like that again?" he asked.

Fred shrugged his shoulders. "No way to know. I doubt it, but I'd sure as heck rope up and have my hammer cocked. Remember what I told you yesterday."

As Ben tightened the cinch, he went through his mental checklist. *Left hand, Cheyenne roll. Right hand, rope. Elbows in. Chin down. Sit deep. Relax.*

"I'll try," said Ben with a shaky laugh. He turned to Soapsuds, gathered up his reins, and reached for the stirrup.

"Just put a toe in the stirrup, so you don't get hung up if he moves off. When you get on, don't fart around. Be ready if he comes uncorked."

As Ben stepped up in the stirrup, Soapsuds threw his head up and shied away.

Ben slipped his toe out and held onto his McCarty. "Whoa," he groaned, willing himself not to rub his aching hip.

"Just start over," Fred said. "Shorten your left rein so if he moves, he comes around toward you. Wait to throw your leg over until he stops moving."

This time when the colt moved, Ben was able to pull himself into the stirrup, hugging the horn until the colt stopped. Then he quickly threw his leg over and picked up his right stirrup.

Soapsuds snorted and minced around in little quick steps before coming to a stop. Ben braced himself against the pain in his hip.

"Hmph," Fred grunted. "Pay attention, he's got a little kink in his tail."

Good thing Fred doesn't know why Soapsuds is acting like this.

"You're tense. Relax," instructed Fred, "and ask him to move his feet."

You bet I'm tense, my hip is killing me.

Ben kicked his heels into the colt's ribs, and Soapsuds squirted forward. Ben grabbed leather, trying to keep his balance.

"Hey, hey, hey!" Fred yelled. "You're rammin' and jammin' again. Remember when I jabbed you in the side?"

Ben grimaced. "Oh, yeah...it's hard to break a habit."

This time he asked the colt lightly with his legs. Soapsuds threw his head up as he stepped forward, then shook it sideways.

"Your reins are too tight. You're stepping on the gas and the brakes at the same time."

Ben frowned, and then he nodded as he pictured himself driving. The colt felt tighter than he had on their first ride, and Ben knew why.

"Give him more slack. Trust him a little, so he can trust you. Just look where you want to go."

Nervously Ben fed out a little more rein, not at all sure that he trusted the colt.

"There, now he's starting to relax and work his mouth."

Soapsuds broke into a fast trot after a few steps. Ben pulled his reins sharply.

"Don't pull on his mouth—you'll make it hard. Take him around in a circle with one rein and just go with him until he walks. Did you feel him building up? Next time, head that off before it starts."

"Before it starts? How?" Ben listened, half confused, as Fred lectured.

"A horse has to get ready before he does anything. Feel what his feet are doing. Just go with him at first. Pretty soon he'll be going along with you. You want him relaxed and confident—not worried about your hands."

Ben gave the colt more slack, thinking about his hands, thinking about the colt's feet, thinking about his attitude, thinking about "what if he bucks?" And trying to be relaxed and trust the colt.

"Man, I never knew you had to think about so many things at once," he said.

Fred returned to the center of the corral and stopped

his horse, watching Ben.

"Ask him to walk out faster, until he breaks into a trot. That's it. Then slow your body rhythm back down to a walk. There!"

As Ben gave more slack, the colt's head began swinging easily, left and right, with the slack reins swinging from side to side. Ben's body began to move in rhythm with the horse.

So many things I never noticed before about how a horse moves.

"You're looking good, boy," said Fred. "Now make a big figure-eight across the pen and go the other way."

Ben started to pick up a rein. Fred called, "Don't even rein him. Just look where you want to go. Turn your whole body. Point your bellybutton and tell him to keep moving his feet."

Ben laughed, turning his body and looking. As the colt picked up the change of direction, Ben felt a warm glow. For the first time, he had an idea of how Fred had handled Black Bob without seeming to rein him.

"Look at the attitude on that colt," said Fred. "He's plumb relaxed. That's what we want."

Ben wasn't sure which felt better—Fred's praise, or the colt underneath him.

"Make sure you get his attention before you ask him to do something. Jiggle your left stirrup, or your left rein, till you see him start to look to the left. Now you're ready to take him to the left."

Ben obeyed. Like magic, Soapsuds looked to the left,

just like Fred said he would, and he began to come around to the left before Ben even reined him. *I wish I had named him Magic!*

"Turn and look at the barn. Use your seat, bring up his life with your legs. Help him just a little with the rein."

The colt wanted to stop as Ben turned him toward the fence. Bumping with his legs, Ben felt the colt come around on his hindquarters. He grinned.

"I've ridden since I was a kid, but old Whitey never felt like this."

"Your body gets ready, and he feels that. Pretty soon, you just *think* about what you want him to do, and he'll do it."

"Aw, I can't believe *that*," Ben said with a snort.

He hauled back on the reins and pulled the colt to a stop.

"Dang it, you're rammin' and jammin' again. Don't pull on his mouth," Fred scolded.

He rode ahead of Ben and demonstrated. "Just shorten your reins and stop your body, like this. That's how you keep his mouth light."

Ben tried it. "It's like magic!"

Fred snorted. "Magic? Any horse will do this. You're feeling of him, and he's feeling of you."

Again Ben remembered watching Fred on Black Bob, how he had done everything without seeming to use his reins. Excitement sizzled inside him as he imagined riding Soapsuds like that some day.

Fred reined his horse to a stop at the gate and stepped

off. "That's enough for today. Put him up while he's doing good."

"Already?" Ben complained.

Fred opened the gate. "Yep, I think that colt may have a bit of *po-ten-tial.*" He emphasized each syllable.

Leading Soapsuds out, Ben glowed with pride. Not that it was his colt, of course. But he felt as proud as if Soapsuds were still his. He ached with happiness and sadness at the same time.

Fred, leading Black Bob, closed the gate. "Yep, maybe I'll make a buckaroo out of you yet, son."

Son? Is he wishing his real son were here instead of me? Feeling self-conscious, Ben didn't say anything. He'd never heard Fred talk so much before.

Fred's really not too bad a guy, he thought as he unsaddled Soapsuds, brushed him and put him up. *I wonder what kind of a dad he used to be? Maybe he only got grouchy after he lost his wife and kid. He even gave me a compliment. That's more than my dad did.*

With a twinge of guilt, he realized he was comparing Fred and his dad. His dad had always been his hero. He always would be. Now Ben looked up to Fred too, but...it seemed to make his dad mad. Did that mean it was wrong?

Chapter 12

The next morning, Ben shivered as he watched the school bus approach. Brakes squealing, it pulled up at the mailbox of the Circle A Ranch. With a whoosh, the door opened and Ben clumped up the steps and down the aisle.

He flopped down into the long back seat, which pretty much belonged to the upper-grade boys. The three-room school had about thirty students this year, with Ben's upper-grade room being fifth through eighth. High school kids faced the long bus ride to Elko.

However, Ben's mind remained back at the ranch, on everything that was bugging him: grouchy old Fred, the argument he had overheard between his parents, the ride he had snuck, and coming off Soapsuds. Restless and impatient, he struggled through the day. Finally three o'clock rolled around, and so did the school bus. He couldn't wait to get home and ride.

Ignoring the conversation of his buddies, and lost in his own thoughts, he stared out the window, remembering how it felt to ride Soapsuds. Better than he had ever dreamed.

"What's the matter with you?" asked Derek. "You in love or something?"

Ben shot Derek a dirty look. "Shut up, moron."

"Lucas is in love! Lucas has a girlfriend!" yelled Derek gleefully.

Slouching down in his seat, Ben ignored the stares and jeers of his friends. *Well, maybe it IS something like being in love.*

Ben had always dreamed about riding Soapsuds, but now his dreams often included Black Bob. Someday he would ride Soapsuds like that.

He pictured himself on the gray and white colt, his arms crossed on his chest, the reins draped over the horn. Like magic, Soapsuds would spin, stop, back up. Ben could hardly wait. How long would it take?

The bus let him off where his red four-wheeler waited for him at the mailbox. He roared full-throttle down the long driveway, skidding around curves, jumping over humps, swerving to avoid potholes. He stopped twice to open and shut barb wire gates along the way.

He loved that strong pungent scent of the endless waves of gray-green sagebrush. His dad said it was the smell of Nevada. Ben imagined himself trotting Soapsuds through the sagebrush, dodging badger holes, following the little trails made by coyotes and cattle.

Rounding the last curve, he caught sight of Fred's pickup by the corrals and the skinny old man in the slouchy black hat getting into his truck. Seeing Ben, he nodded and waved in his usual way—both hands on the top of the steering wheel, lazily raising one finger.

As soon as Fred disappeared, Ben cranked the

handlebars and gunned the motor. Pleased with all the noise and dust, he headed home.

When his dad drove up, Ben ran out to meet him. They leaned on the pickup for a while, talking about their day. Ben loved it when his dad took time alone with him like this. Pete started talking about something that had happened that day with the horse he'd been riding.

Ben furrowed his eyebrows, trying to follow his dad's line of reasoning.

"Say you try to turn him to the right, but he ignores you. You *make* him go to the right, no matter how firm you have to get."

Ben snorted. "A horse is so strong, he's going to win if he wants to. How can you make him?"

"What if a cliff is straight ahead, or a barb wire fence, or a 2000-pound bull, slinging his horns and blowing snot? A horse that's gotten his own way will ignore you every chance he gets, because he's learned that he can."

They started toward the house. "If you don't teach a horse to respect you, to obey, someday he just may get you killed. If you let him win, the next time he decides to try you, you'll have an even bigger fight."

Pete opened the kitchen door and led the way in. "Outsmart him. If you don't let him win, he won't know he's strong enough to win."

He put down his thermos and headed for the living room. Ben sat down at the kitchen table, where he'd piled his books earlier. His dad did have some good ideas about horses, he had to admit.

Sighing, Ben tried to sort out his confused thoughts. His dad had taught him to ride and much more. Ben called him a "walking encyclopedia." He'd started colts, cowboyed, rodeoed, shod horses, and doctored sick horses. He knew about bloodlines, saddles, bridles, bits, ropes, and knots. Ben had soaked it all in, never questioning.

He compared his dad's way to Fred's way. Just because Fred learned different ways than Pete didn't make Pete wrong about everything. That's what confused Ben. Now he had to sort things out for himself. Whose way was right?

I'm not a little kid anymore. It's not like I have to do everything in life exactly like Dad, do I? Can't I be like both of them?

Chapter 13

The next day after school, Ben found Black Bob standing saddled at the tie rack. Ben poked his head in the door of the barn, looking around. Fred emerged from the tack room.

"Well, what are you doing just standing there? Get that colt of yours saddled up," he growled.

Startled, Ben grabbed a halter and rope and headed for the corral.

Geez, what a grouch! But...he said "that colt of yours." What's THAT supposed to mean? Is he thinking, maybe, of giving him back to me? Like, maybe if I do a good job starting him?

His heart skipped a beat, and his head floated like a balloon. Catching the colt easily, he haltered him and led him to the tie rack.

Man, Fred is a weird guy to be friends with. You can't ever tell if he's mad or what. Maybe he's been grouchy for so long, he just doesn't know how to be nice.

As he began brushing Soapsuds, Fred strolled over and ran his hand lazily along the colt's rump.

"Nice build, long hip, straight legs. And a good

disposition to boot. I think he's gonna be a double-good son-of-a-gun."

Brushing slowly with his right hand, Ben slid his left hand along behind the brush, noticing the winter coat already coming on.

"My dad never let me pet the horses, even my own colt." He savored the sound of those words: "my own colt." He hoped that by saying them, he might encourage Fred to think in that direction. "He says, dogs and cats are for pets. Horses are for work."

"Well, I might agree with him there," said Fred. "If you make a pet out of him, you might make him dull. I want him to notice and respond to my every move."

As Ben saddled the colt, Fred untied the black and stepped on. He lifted his reins slightly. Black Bob's neck arched a little and his nose tucked. Ears flicking back and forth, he glided forward easily. Ben hadn't seen Fred move, but now he knew that Fred had just tightened his legs and shifted his weight.

"Now finish getting that colt saddled up," Fred said impatiently. "Hustle!"

Ben hurried off to get his saddle, making a face at Fred. But he couldn't stay mad. He wanted to impress Fred so he'd think that Ben deserved to get his colt back.

"Okay. Get on that colt, and we'll go for a trot out through the sagebrush."

As they shut the last gate behind them, Fred said, "Don't forget you're on a green colt. This is his first time outside. Be ready for anything."

Don't forget? That was all Ben could think about. The way Soapsuds bucked that first day. The way he spun out from under him when he snuck that moonlit ride.

Be ready for anything. Old rusty strands of barb wire that might be hiding in the sagebrush. Badger holes. Walmart sacks. Jackrabbits, pheasants, deer—the colt could spook at anything.

Ben went through his mental checklist: hands, legs, seat, relax, trust your horse. And if he bucks: elbows in, chin down, sit deep, go for the rope and the cantle. And relax. *How can you make yourself relax?* he wondered.

As if reading his mind again, Fred said, "There's lots of wide open space out here. No telling how this bugger will act. If he gets excited and takes off with you, remember, he can't run faster than you can ride. Do this."

He demonstrated. "Shorten up one rein and let him run into that bit so he comes around in a circle. He's stronger than you. Don't get in a fight with him."

Ben nodded, remembering his dad's advice: "Outsmart him. Don't let him know he's strong enough to win." *They're both saying the same thing. Hmm.*

They headed down a dirt road and then cut out through the sagebrush.

"Keep his mind busy, direct those feet, and he won't have time to think about bucking you off. Weave in and out around this sagebrush. That'll give him a job to do."

Soapsuds responded to Ben's legs, flicking his ears back and forth as Ben got his attention on the left and then on the right. He tried to be prepared for the unexpected—

especially one of those spins that Ben knew all too well.

The late afternoon sunlight was thin and cold as the sun began to sink behind the mountains. The icy wind bit Ben's ears and fingers, making his nose tingle. He inhaled deeply, grinning. *Maybe I AM in love. If being in love is better than this, it must be pretty good.*

"Let me ride him home," said Fred, coming up alongside him. "Here, you ride Bob. It'll be good for you."

They traded horses, adjusting their stirrups and checking their cinches before remounting. The colt didn't want to stand still for Fred to get on. Ben felt guilty, remembering how he had lunged at Soapsuds from the fence and scared him.

"Whoa there, you old Soap Scum," Fred growled, shortening his reins and reaching again for the stirrup.

Soapsuds felt fresh and strong, but the black rode as smooth as chocolate pudding. Like the difference between a pickup and a sports car. He seemed to read Ben's mind—just like Fred did.

Watching Fred on Soapsuds, Ben suddenly felt jealous. He noticed how the colt seemed to melt in Fred's hands.

Then an ugly new thought popped into his head.

He's been planning all along on training Soapsuds himself! He's just been USING me, making me get on first, to make sure HE doesn't get bucked off. And now that he sees everything is okay, he's going to take over. No wonder he's always so grouchy to me. He doesn't really want me riding his colt. He was just too chicken to start him alone.

Ben rode out ahead of Fred the rest of the way back.

He didn't want to hear anything else Fred might have to say, and it hurt to see someone on his colt.

I know he's Fred's colt now, but I don't want him to care for anyone but ME!

Chapter 14

The next afternoon, Ben tried to stay mad at Fred, but the minute he caught the colt, his hurt feelings vanished. Eager for another lesson, he and Soapsuds met Fred in the arena. Fred put Black Bob straight into a lope and then slid him to a stop in front of Ben and Soapsuds, pivoting completely around in a circle.

"See? A cowhorse is an athlete. He needs to move quickly in any direction, to stop and turn a cow. When that cow ducks in front of him, I want him to turn so fast that he meets himself coming the other way."

He stroked the horse's neck. "I can put his feet anywhere I want. Why, he'd step in a hot bear track for me, if I asked him to."

Ben hooted. "Yeah, right."

Fred patted Black Bob. "I know my horse. He trusts me."

Still skeptical, Ben shook his head.

"Well, enough of this," said Fred, leading the way out the gate. "Take that potlikker out for a little trot through the sagebrush and then put him up."

"You coming?" asked Ben.

"Naw. You'll be fine. Just keep him lined out, don't go too far, and don't do anything stupid."

He paused, then added, "If I see any buzzards circling, I'll come looking for you."

"Huh? Buzzards? But buzzards only circle around stuff that's...oh, I get it," Ben said. He added, "Whatever... don't worry," and turned Soapsuds away from the barn.

Cool, he thought, swelling with pride. *Fred thinks I can handle a green colt outside all by myself!*

Confidently, he squeezed Soapsuds into a trot, heading the colt down a familiar trail that led out through the sagebrush.

He had spent lots of time out here playing as a kid. *Hmm, it should be around here somewhere...yep, it's still there!* He rode past one of the many sagebrush forts he had built a few years ago. Funny...he used to be so proud of them, but now they appeared almost childish to him.

As Soapsuds settled down, Ben quickly went through his mental checklist: *Sit deep, think about hands, think about legs, relax. Be ready if he bucks—elbows in, go for my rope and my cantle.*

The late afternoon air was brisk, and Ben wished he'd worn gloves. His breath clouded before him, and he could see his horse's breath coming in short puffs. Their long shadows melted away as the late-afternoon sun slipped behind a cloud.

Oh, and watch for badger holes. A horse could drop to his chest and break a leg. Like that horse that died. Which is why Soapsuds belongs to Fred.

Ben felt the knife twist in his chest. *But maybe, if I do a good job...*

Tightening his legs, he leaned forward and sucked in his breath as Soapsuds broke into a fast lope.

The smell of sagebrush, the rhythm of hoof beats, the creak of saddle leather, the taste of dust, the soft snorty breathing of his horse—it was perfect.

The cattle trail crossed a rise and then descended. The distant buildings vanished behind them. Just sagebrush and mountains filled the horizon.

This is how it must have looked when the first people came to this valley, he thought. *I wish I'd been born 150 years ago.*

"Ben Lucas...fearless mountain man, cattle king, famous horseman," people were saying, "and his legendary gray horse, Soapsuds!"

For a moment, Ben wished he'd named the colt something more romantic. *I should've named him* Magic. *Oh well, Dad would think that's corny.*

His pretend-life flashed through his mind like a video: Ben Lucas. Staking out a homestead claim. Turning it into a great cattle empire. His herds of fat white-faced cattle scattered across the whole valley. His famous home-bred horses known far and wide. His livestock wearing his own brand...

From behind a tall sagebrush, a black cow lurched to her feet. She lowered her head and bawled, slinging her horns.

Soapsuds snorted and twisted sideways in mid-stride,

bringing Ben partly back to earth as he grabbed leather. Then, with that treacherous spin, he sent Ben the rest of the way to earth.

Ben's hand automatically grabbed the McCarty tucked in his belt—a move he had practiced often in his mind.

Whack! He landed on his back, his head whipping to the ground. Scratchy sagebrush clawed his face.

"Dang...my head..." Clutching his McCarty, he struggled painfully to his feet, calling softly, "Whoa, easy there, easy boy."

The colt stood stiffly at the end of the rope. *Good thing I've still got a hold of him.*

He gently slid his hand up the rope, crooning softly to his horse. Soapsuds whooshed his breath through his flared nostrils and then stepped forward uncertainly, his eyes big. Ben rubbed his face and talked to him softly. The cow trotted off, bawling.

"That a boy, that's it," he murmured. "What's wrong with you, you sorry excuse for a cowhorse?"

He slid his hand up behind the colt's ears and rubbed. Soapsuds relaxed, lowered his head, and snuffed Ben's arm.

"Ain't you ever seen a cow before?" he went on in a soothing monotone. "Doggone you...oh my aching neck... stand still now..."

He ran his hand along the colt's neck, rubbing the base of his mane. Finally he moved to his shoulder.

Gathering up his reins, he held them snugly so the colt wouldn't step away. Still talking, he took the stirrup and stuck his toe in. Pain shot through his back, and he let his foot slide out. He groaned, his head reeling.

Dang, that hurt! I don't think anything's broken. Did Dad really manage to get on with a broken bone? I guess I can do this if I just try harder.

Steadying himself, he tried again, grabbing the saddle with both hands and stiffly swinging up, panting from pain. The quick movement made him dizzy. His head felt like someone had used it for batting practice.

"Okay, let's go now. Nice and easy."

Tucking his McCarty under his belt, he walked Soapsuds toward home.

Man, I sure didn't see that coming, thought Ben, angry at himself. *I should've been paying attention, not daydreaming.* He rubbed his neck and groaned again. *What an idiot.*

Keeping the colt's mind busy, he zig-zagged around sagebrush. As they trotted, walked, stopped, and turned, he worked on using his seat and legs instead of relying on his reins only.

He talked to Soapsuds to cover his nervous thoughts. "This is what I should've been doing all along—all that stuff Fred's been trying to teach me. I thought I was ready if you bucked, but man, I sure wasn't ready for that nasty spin of yours!"

He relived the dizzying spin and remembered Fred's words: "When that cow ducks in front of him, I want him to turn so fast that he meets himself coming the other way."

Well, that's what happened, alright. I wonder if Fred knows you can move like that? He seems to know everything, whether I tell him or not.

As they approached the barn, Ben could see Fred's pickup. *Dang. He WOULD have to be there. He's never going to let me ride Soapsuds again.* Ben chewed on his lip.

Riding the colt up to the tie rack, he clumsily dismounted, groaning under his breath. Fred glanced up from where he was forking hay into the mangers at one side of the corral. Leaning on the pitchfork handle, he watched Ben move around the colt, undoing the cinch.

Ben stumped toward the tack room, packing the big stock saddle. Stumbling over the door sill, he fell on top of the saddle. He turned to see Fred standing over him.

"That colt iron you out, son?"

Ben hesitated only briefly before lying again. "No. We played pretty rough at school today. It's just catching up with me now." He grinned and rubbed his back.

Fred kept looking at him with those prying eyes. Ben knew he knew, but Fred said nothing.

How does he know?

Fred half-smiled over to one side of his mouth.

Trying not to let his eyes admit anything, Ben said, "Well, I better get going."

Fred stepped aside as Ben hurried past him, grabbing a brush from the milk crate by the door, and the hoof pick from the nail on the wall. He quickly brushed down the colt, checked each foot for rocks, and then turned him into the corral.

On his four-wheeler, he gunned the motor and cranked the handlebars around, groaning and gritting his teeth.

Might as well just head on down to the pasture and feed.

When Ben came in for dinner, his dad looked up from the kitchen table where he sat reading the mail.

"What're you gimping around for?" he asked, frowning.

"Oh, I kind of had a...wreck," he said. As he expected, his dad's eyes narrowed and followed him across the room. He hung his jacket on the coat rack by the door.

"I came off..." he hesitated, "...my four-wheeler, when I went to feed."

Lying had never been part of Ben's nature, but it was just a little fib. And each fib got a little easier to tell.

Pete made a face and let out his breath noisily.

"I tried to jump a ditch."

"That's a dang poor way to treat that machine," snapped his dad.

Ben bit his lip. *Yeah, worry about the machine, but don't bother yourself about whether or not I got hurt.*

His mom stood at the counter, tearing up lettuce for a salad. She turned, her eyes worried.

"Are you okay?"

"Yeah." He rubbed his neck.

"Maybe you'd better not ride that colt tomorrow."

"I'm fine, Mom." He sighed as dramatically as he could. *Man! I HATE to be treated like a little kid.*

His mom turned again, her eyes traveling from Pete to Ben. She too sighed and turned back to her salad. "Dinner's about ready."

The plates and utensils waited in a stack at one end of the table. Ben slapped them down in front of each chair, drawing another glance from his mother, which he ignored.

He doesn't care if I get hurt, he tells me how to start the colt, he acts like I don't know anything—why can't he let me do things my own way?

Chapter 15

"We'll put thirty rides on him, then turn him out 'til next year..." Ben didn't like to think about Fred's words. The days passed way too fast. Fortunately the weather held. Thanks to the lack of snow, Ben could ride most days. The cold and the wind didn't bother him much.

Usually Fred rode with him, giving him pointers on horsemanship; sometimes he rode alone. Never too far, maybe a few miles—lots of long trotting, or moving a few cows.

Ben loved the powerful surge of the colt's lope but followed Fred's orders to build him up with trotting. After all, it *was* Fred's colt, not Ben's. Ben wanted to do his best, hoping Fred would notice and realize he was worthy of having the colt back. He couldn't stand to think about Soapsuds being in someone's string next year.

How would they ride him? Would they jerk and spur? What if my dad got the colt?

Ben knew his dad could be pretty rough with a horse. What could he do about it? Would he have the nerve to try to change his dad's ways, to try to help him see that Soapsuds didn't need to be yanked and spurred?

As Ben unsaddled the colt after a good ride, he counted. *Less than a week...will Saturday be it?*

While waiting for dinner, Pete looked up the number for the Elko fire station. As he dialed, Ben whispered excitedly, "Put it on speaker phone, Dad!"

Pete nodded and pushed the button.

"Hi, this is Pete Lucas over here at the Greeley Volunteer Fire Department. Hey, you got that truck in yet?"

"Hi, Pete. It just came in yesterday—I've got a note right here to call you. Heavy brush truck, 1968 Ford F800, four-wheel-drive. How does that sound?"

"Perfect!"

"It's sitting outside, waiting for someone to come get it."

"Can we pick it up tomorrow, late afternoon?"

"Sure thing!"

"Great, my boy and I will be there about 4:00 or so. Will you have time to show us how it works?"

"Yep, we'll give you a quick tour of the truck."

"Okay, see you then." Pete hung up the phone.

Ben noticed that his dad said "show us," not "show me." That made him feel important and manly. He loved doing man-stuff with his dad. He could hardly wait to see the truck.

"Suz, you got some chores to do in town? You can drop us off at the firehouse, run around town a bit, and then follow us home."

"You know I've always got a list here on the side of the fridge." She pulled it from the magnet. "It's getting pretty long—I haven't been to town for a few weeks. And I need to go to the bank too."

"Okay, it's settled then. I'll make sure I'm back at the house early tomorrow. Ben, instead of you riding the bus home, we'll just pick you up at school and leave straight from there."

"Are you going to let the other guys know about the truck?" asked Susie.

"Yeah, I'll make a few calls this evening. We need to plan a meeting now that we've got the truck."

Tuesday flew by as Ben worked extra hard all day so he wouldn't have any homework that night. When the bell rang at 3:00, he turned in his last paper and grabbed his backpack.

"You coming over today to work on our report?" asked Derek, bumping him out of the way to get through the door first.

Ben bumped him back, even harder. "Maybe tomorrow. Me and my dad are going to Elko to pick up the fire truck."

"Oh, man, can I come too?"

"No!" Ben laughed and swaggered, pointing a jeering finger in Derek's face. "*I'm* going to see it first! I'm going to ride in it! Hahaha!"

Derek faked a punch, jabbed Ben in the belly, and then danced away as Ben tried to trip him.

"No fighting!" yelled a teacher.

"We're not fighting!" they both yelled back.

"Okay," Derek said, "see you tomorrow then."

Ben headed toward the parking lot as Derek joined

the bus line. His mom opened the pickup door and scooted toward Pete as Ben tossed his backpack in the back on top of the water jug, empty ice chests, and the extra can of diesel fuel. He crawled in beside her.

"Did you bring me a snack? What smells so good?"

As they pulled out onto the road, Susie laughed. "I brought us a little something to eat on the way."

She reached into the sack on her lap and pulled out some tin foil packages. Partly peeling back the foil, she handed one to Pete and one to Ben.

"Mmm, cinnamon rolls—my favorite! And they're still warm!"

Pete took a huge bite and then mumbled with his mouth full, "I hope you brought napkins."

"Thanks, Mom, you're the best!"

Ben smooshed the sweet spicy bread against the roof of his mouth, hardly bothering to chew. He finished his roll in a few big bites, eyeing the bag. "Got any more hiding in there?"

Susie laughed as Pete and Ben held out their hands expectantly. She dug in the sack for more.

"Good thing I was in the mood to bake today. I figured you guys would both be hungry."

Ben wolfed down another one as his mom nibbled on hers. Smacking his lips noisily, he reached for the sack and peered in.

"Got anything to drink in there? Oh, milk! Nothing like cold milk to wash down a warm gooey cinnamon roll."

"Ready for some coffee, dear?" she asked Pete,

reaching under the seat for the thermos.

"Just a little—half a snort," he said, watching her pour. "I'm trying to drive!" She carefully handed him the thermos cup.

The rich aroma of coffee wafted through the truck. Even though Ben didn't care for the taste of coffee, the smell made him feel warm all over.

He loved going to town with his folks and hanging out with his dad. His mom always did cool stuff like this when they traveled.

The pickup flew down the long straight road. On either side of the valley, snow-topped mountain ranges rose like friendly giants watching over the little people at their feet.

When they passed an occasional ranch road, a bike, a four-wheeler, or even an old pickup waited at the mailbox for kids, who, like Ben, drove home from the long school bus ride. A few mothers waited in vehicles.

As a white pickup passed them going the other way, everyone waved at each other.

"James and his mom are coming back from Elko," Ben said. "He told us he had a doctor's appointment."

"Good thing you wanted to go on a Tuesday, so I could go too," Susie said.

To supplement their modest income, she drove the mail truck on Monday, Wednesday, and Friday to the next valley over. That valley had no post office—too few people, and too far out. She also did the bookkeeping for the ranch.

"And I'm out of lots of stuff. I don't like to cut things

that close, especially in case we get unexpected company."

"Hey, do you have time to swing by the feed store and pick me up some horseshoes and a box of nails?" asked Pete. Most buckaroos did their own shoeing.

Susie pulled her list out of her purse. "Yeah, I think I can get there before they close. What size shoes and how many?"

"A set of double oughts—that colt I just started has pretty small feet. Make sure you get fronts and hinds— they're different, you know."

She wrote it down and checked over her list. "Bank, feed store, grocery store. And I'll stop by the thrift store and pick you up some work shirts." She got out her checkbook and calculator and started working on something.

Ben spotted some antelope out in the sagebrush. Cattle grazed on the stubble of scattered alfalfa fields.

Now that nights had been freezing for a while, the yellow flowers that made his mother sneeze no longer covered the rabbitbrush. In the fall they turned to pale golden puffballs that glowed almost silver in the low rays of the late afternoon sun.

The Silver State. Ben pondered the title. *Silver mines. Silver sagebrush.* He pictured the gray and white colt. Almost silver. Not quite.

"There goes the train," Pete said. Then, pointing, "And someone's trailing some cattle."

Ben spotted the distant thread of dust. Dark specks formed a long line, with a couple of taller specks behind them.

"It's such big country," Susie mused. "When we first came here, it almost scared me. So empty and ugly. No trees. So far from everything—stores, hospital, people."

"That's funny," Pete said. "When I go to California, it almost scares *me!* Too many people, cars, buildings. Got to lock your doors. Can't see the blue sky or the mountains."

"Well, that's the way I feel now too. This wild barren sagebrush country does grow on you. I'm so glad you brought me here!" Susie leaned over and gave him a kiss on the cheek.

Ben groaned. "Gross!" he said, looking the other way.

When they arrived at the firehouse, Pete and Ben got out, and Susie slid over behind the wheel.

"Call me on the cell phone when you're about done here," she reminded them. She eased the pickup back onto the road as they waved goodbye.

Chapter 16

A rough-looking guy with a bristly gray buzz-cut met Pete and Ben at the firehouse door. He looked like a retired football coach—broad and brawny.

Reaching for Pete's outstretched hand, he said, "You must be Pete Lucas. I'm the fire chief, Hank Curtis."

"Glad to meet you. This is my boy, Ben."

Ben stuck out his hand. Hank had a killer grip.

"I'll walk you guys through this baby. You want to take notes?" He grabbed a clipboard and pen from his desk.

Ben reached for them, saying, "I'll handle that."

Hank nodded approvingly. "Good lad."

They walked out to the truck. "Your paperwork is in the envelope on the seat, your manuals are all in the jockey box. Talk to your men about trainings—I'll send out my assistant chief or the captain. Figure out what day and time works for you guys."

Pete nodded, looking to see that Ben wrote it all down. "We've been training some so we'd be ready when we got the truck. We practice putting on and using all our gear. We've already organized a phone chain to contact all our people."

"Good. To work on the engine, tip this lever. It takes two guys to tip the hood forward."

They tipped it up and then back down.

Three ladders hung on hooks along the passenger side. "These two are extension ladders. This is a roof ladder."

He pointed to a group of gauges and levers on the driver's side, just past the cab. "Your pump panel is right back here. This pump will run about 1,000 gallons per minute. You've got a separate engine in the box behind this panel to run the pump. Let's fire this baby up."

He climbed into the cab and turned the ignition switch on, letting the noisy truck run while he jumped out, flipped the toggle switch on the fuel pump, and pushed the starter button.

The pump engine howled to life. Ben wanted to clap his hands over his ears. Instead, he scribbled frantically while Hank walked Pete through the various gauges.

Hank killed the motor. "Put your best man on this pump control panel—he'll be your engineer. If you've got too much pressure going, the hoses jump around and are hard to control. If they jerk out of your hands, they can flip around and get someone hurt."

"How do you keep that from happening?" Pete asked.

Hank grabbed a lever. "Say you're running both hoses on 100 pounds of pressure, and one nozzle gets shut off, the other one jumps to maybe 150 pounds. Watch these gauges, and adjust the pressure up or down as it varies between the two hoses. It takes quite a bit of practice."

Pete grunted. "Hm."

"Okay, we need to learn to take down these hoses. You got two sets of cross-lays here, 200 feet each, enough to get you around a house either way. Put your arm through this loop, grab the nozzle and pull it all down *hard*."

Ben studied the way the men worked with the heavy hose. He drew little pictures beside his notes. It was important to get it just right. His dad would need to explain everything to the other men.

"When you're done, lay the hose out straight and take the nozzle off. Start at the truck, put the hose over your shoulder, and strip it—walk down the hose with both hands squeezing the water out."

He and Pete pretended to strip the hose and lay it back in the truck.

"Wear gloves—the hose will be dirty, muddy, and full of stickers."

They poked around some more, looking at all the features of the truck, talking about fire-fighting strategy. Ben's hand ached from writing.

"Make sure you don't park this baby outside, now that nights are freezing."

Pete nodded. "Until we get a fire house, we'll use a barn—no problem there."

Finally Pete pointed to the office. "Can we use your phone? We'll go eat, then come back and get the truck."

"Sure, come on in." They all trooped inside.

"Ben, tell Mom we're almost ready." While Ben called, Pete signed papers. They waited out at the truck, going over the manuals until Susie drove up.

After they ate and drove back to the firehouse, Pete told her, "We've got a full tank of fuel, but this rig only gets about three miles per gallon, and I don't even know if the gauges work. Just follow us home, to be on the safe side. There's extra diesel in the back."

Noticing all the boxes and bags back there, he growled, "Sheesh, how much did you buy? Looks like enough to feed half of Greeley."

Ben thought, *Not a good way to start the trip home. Now he's in a mood just because he's a little worried about driving this thing. I hope he doesn't ruin my first ride in the fire truck.*

Pete cranked the motor until it caught. "Okay, now where the heck are the headlights?"

He fumbled around, accidentally turned on the windshield wipers and then the turn signal. He muttered and cussed under his breath.

"Now *where* are the brights? I can't be fiddling with this stuff when we're going through town." The overhead lights in the cab flashed on. "For cryin' out loud!"

Ben held his breath, waiting for his dad to get organized.

"Sheesh! Too many gadgets on this danged truck."

Pete shifted into gear. Ben stiffened at the grinding sound. The truck jerked forward.

Finally, they were on the road.

"Where's your mom?"

Ben looked over his shoulder. "She's right there. Don't worry."

By the time they hit the freeway, Pete managed to shift just a little smoother.

"Man, I can't get the feel of this clutch," he growled.

"Can you turn on the heater?" Ben asked after a while. "It's freezing in here."

Pete snapped, "Can't you see I've got my hands full? Figure it out."

Ben fiddled with the dials until he had some heat going. *So much for my fun adventure.*

They rode along in silence for a while. Ben thought maybe he ought to try to start a conversation.

"Dad, about the colt…"

"Yeah," interrupted his dad, "I've been thinking about those colts. Glad you brought it up."

That's not what I wanted to talk about, Ben silently complained. *I want to talk about Soapsuds!*

"Those colts need started. I've been thinking we need to set a day for you to buck them out."

Ben tensed up.

"I'm thinking Sunday afternoon. How does that sound?"

Sunday was only five days away. Ben shrugged his shoulders and answered half-heartedly, "I guess."

"Better tell Derek. You asked him to come and watch."

"No, I didn't!" Ben said indignantly. "He invited himself." Having Derek watch would only make it worse.

"You let that Derek push you around too much. Like today when we picked you up. He shoved you and punched you, and you didn't do anything about it. Don't take that kind of garbage from him."

"*Dad!* We were just playing around! And anyhow, I dish it back to him. He always starts it, but I don't let him take advantage of me."

"It didn't look like that to me. Looks like he's walking all over you."

Ben bit his lip and looked away. *There he goes again. Always hinting that I'm not tough enough.*

They drove along in silence for a while. Ben decided to try again.

"Dad, I need to go to Derek's after school tomorrow. We're working on a report together."

Pete replied, "Okay, yeah, I guess..." Then he added, "But try not to get into any trouble."

Sheesh! thought Ben. *He wants me to be tough, he doesn't want me to let Derek push me around, but he just assumes I'm going to get into trouble. I don't get it.*

"Thanks, Dad," he mumbled with a touch of sarcasm.

Seems to me he *used to get into lots of trouble when HE was a kid. He told me about stuff he did. I guess that's different.*

Bitter thoughts piled up in Ben's mind like rumbling thunderheads.

Trying to talk to him is just a waste of time.

Dark silence filled the cab. The big truck echoed the rumbling inside Ben's head.

Chapter 17

Missing Wednesday's ride would now make Sunday their last. After school, Ben threw his backpack into the box on the back of his four-wheeler and headed for Derek's house, about eight miles away. Dirt roads crisscrossed the valley, winding through the sagebrush. Ben knew most of them as well as he knew the freckles on his nose.

When he was just a kid, he explored them on his bike, but ever since his grandparents gave him the red four-wheeler, he spent hours out in the brush. Off by himself with not a person or house in sight, he felt grown up.

He had even driven them in the old truck. But today his dad needed that truck, so the four-wheeler would do. Ben knew the road well enough to take each bump and curve just as fast as he could, without losing control.

Suddenly Ben grabbed the brake lever hard, his heart pounding. Just in front of him, one strand of barb wire stretched across the road. Spewing dirt into the air, the ATV skidded and slid toward the deadly wire. Ben cranked the handlebars, swerving out of control. He ducked his head sideways, bracing for the impact. Pain seared his neck. "Aaaagh!"

The four-wheeler stopped in a cloud of dust under the wire. Ben jumped off, clutching the side of his neck.

"*Daaang!*" he yelled.

He stood there in shock, looking at the wire. "Where the heck did *that* come from?"

His knees shook so hard, he could barely stay on his feet. Gingerly removing his hand from his neck, he shuddered at the sight of his own blood.

Instinctively he clapped his hand over his neck again and pressed hard against the pain, hoping to slow the bleeding. Fear and anger surged through his body. He had to get home quickly.

But first he unhooked the deadly wire from the gatepost. There had never been a gate across this road before! And who had ever heard of a single-strand gate? And just high enough that it could have cut his head off if he hadn't seen it in time! What if he hadn't ducked at the last second?

Ben shook with rage. *What dang fool could have done such a STUPID thing?*

He felt in his pocket—yes, a glove. He undid his belt, pulled it off, and tried to fasten the glove in place on his neck. His hands were shaking. But he couldn't buckle it that snug, and it was too stiff to tie.

He thought again...*my shoelace!* He jerked out one of the laces and tied the glove to his neck as tightly as he could stand it. A fleeting picture crossed his mind: tying a handkerchief around Fred's bloody head that day on the mountain.

Driving home seemed to take forever. Weak and shaky from the shock to his body and mind, he couldn't drive as fast as before. His jumbled thoughts raced ahead of the four-wheeler.

What will Mom and Dad say? His dad would probably jump him about driving irresponsibly, even though this wasn't his fault.

He felt tingly and had trouble focusing. *I wonder how bad I'm hurt? What if I don't make it home? Dear God, please help me!*

When he opened the kitchen door, his mother turned from the sink. She gasped, wiping her hands on the towel.

"Ben!" She ran to him and started untying the make-shift bandage. Ben leaned against her and wrapped his arms around her. He'd never been so glad to see his mother.

"Here, sit down. You're white as a ghost. What happened?"

Ben crumpled into a chair. He was so relieved to be home that he almost started crying. As he told the story, his mom removed his bloody jacket and shirt and gently washed his neck, his shoulder, and the cut, just above his collarbone.

Every time she touched the cloth to his wound, Ben flinched, grabbing the edge of the table and gritting his teeth, trying not to cry out.

"I'm sorry...I'm so sorry...just take a breath," she kept saying as she worked calmly and quietly. Ben wanted to just hug her and hug her but he sat as still as he could.

He heard the motor of the old truck. His dad was home.

Pete walked in the door.

"Ben?" He rushed to Ben's side, his face full of concern. "What in the *Sam Hill*?" He peered at Ben's neck and touched him gently.

"It's not too deep," said Susie. "I don't think it's as bad as it looks. Thank the good Lord he got that machine stopped when he did. Another couple inches and I hate to think what could have happened."

Ben retold the story to his dad.

"Jeeee-miny Christmas!" Pete said angrily. "What in dang-nation would possess any person in his right mind to run a damned wire across a road like that?"

"Pete, watch your language!" scolded Susie.

He stomped off to hang up his jacket.

"Do I need to go to the hospital?" Ben asked in a shaky voice.

His dad examined his neck as his mom dabbed it with disinfectant.

"You know, I think you're right, Suz. It's a surface wound, and the bleeding has pretty much stopped. You've cleaned it up good. I can't see that it really needs stitches."

"That's what I was thinking. Why run clear to Elko if they'd just clean and bandage it."

"Well, I've doctored enough cows and horses to have a pretty good idea of how to treat a wound."

He shook Ben by the shoulder playfully. "Well, I think you're going to live, pardner!"

Ben tried to grin. He liked it when his dad called him "pardner."

The phone rang a little later. Susie answered it.

"Oh, hi, Derek...No, Ben won't be coming over today. He isn't feeling well...thanks...bye-bye."

After dinner Pete headed to fire training. The men were anxious to train with the truck, which was parked down in one of the Circle A sheds.

Ben sulked all evening. He worked on his report, trying to keep his mind on his writing. Anger and fear smoldered in his stomach. *What if I hadn't seen it in time? I could be dead! I'm going to find whoever did that!*

On the bus next morning, Ben didn't head for the big back seat where the older boys sat. He didn't want to talk to Derek or James. He didn't feel like laughing or joking around.

Instead, he found an empty seat near the front. With a turtleneck shirt and his jacket collar up around his neck, maybe no one would notice his bandage and ask about it.

He avoided Derek all day. Derek had really been bugging him lately—teasing him about having a girlfriend. Ben had warned him to quit spreading lies, but Derek seemed to enjoy getting a reaction.

He made it through the day without talking much to anyone. At recess he stayed in to work. Finally the three o'clock bell rang, and Ben started for the bus. He looked behind him. *Oh great, here he comes. Just who I don't want to talk to.*

"What are you on the hook about today?" Derek said in an accusing voice.

"Oh, nothing." Ben's voice dripped with sarcasm. "Just

that some *idiot* ran a string of barb wire across the road. I ran into it on my four-wheeler yesterday on the way to your house!"

He threw down his backpack and jerked down the collar of his shirt so Derek could see the bandage. "I could have cut my head off!"

Derek's jaw dropped and the color drained from his face. He threw down his backpack next to Ben's.

Ben glared. "My dad said *someone* is not in his right mind!"

Derek looked away uncomfortably, chewing on his bottom lip.

"What?" demanded Ben. "Do you know who did it?"

Derek gulped. He whispered slowly, "I...I did it."

Ben grabbed him by the shoulders. *"What?"* he burst out. "*What* would you do a stupid thing like that for?"

"My...my dad told me to make a gate across that road— now that the cows are turned out over there. I was in a hurry so...I just ran the one strand. I was going to go back later and...do it better...I forgot...I'm...I'm sorry, man..."

"Well, I took it down before it killed someone!"

"You took it down?" snapped Derek, his eyes flashing. "Oh great! Now those cows are probably all over heck, and my dad is going to kill *me.*"

"If you hadn't been an *idiot* in the first place, that wouldn't have happened!" Ben advanced threateningly.

"Shut up!" yelled Derek, backing away.

By now a group of students had gathered to watch the commotion.

"*You* shut up!" yelled Ben back, giving Derek a hard shove in the chest.

Derek threw a wild punch. Ben ducked, and it glanced off the side of his jaw.

A couple of boys yelled, "Fight! Fight!"

Ben exploded. He smashed his fist into Derek's face. Derek staggered and fell backward.

Chapter 18

"He decked him! Ben decked him!" someone hollered. Everyone crowded around, yelling.

Ben rubbed his jaw as Derek raised himself on one elbow, bleeding from his nose. He moaned, "Ohhhh......my baaaack!" A teacher headed toward them.

Both mothers got a phone call. Fighting equaled an automatic one-day suspension. *It's not fair,* thought Ben. *He hit me first!*

Sitting by himself again on the bus, Ben cooled down on the ride home. He even smiled to himself. *Now Dad will see that I'm tough.*

But Ben's plan backfired. When Pete heard about the fight at dinner, Ben was in more trouble. "You what? You got yourself kicked out of school?"

"You got in fights! You told me so!" said Ben, his face turning hot.

"I never fought at school."

"But, *Dad,* he almost killed me! He deserved it!" His voice cracked. "You always said I should never start a fight, but if someone else started it, I ought to finish it."

"Don't argue with me!"

In the morning his mom smeared his wound with the bag balm they used for first aid, and put on a clean bandage.

"Good, no sign of infection. How does it feel?" she asked.

"Okay, I guess. It hurts when I move my head."

Pete showed no sympathy.

"If you think you're getting a day off today, guess again. You won't be lying around or playing. I'm going to see to it that you work, that's for sure. Then we'll see how you like fighting at school."

"But Dad, my neck hurts!"

"Don't argue!" said his dad. "Tough it out!"

Ben dropped his eyes so his dad couldn't see his expression.

Softening his voice, Pete said, "Fred and I are riding today, but the rest of the crew are working around here. You'll help them all day. I've already talked to them about it."

No one spoke during breakfast. When Ben finished, he sullenly pulled on his jacket and mashed his wide-brimmed black felt hat down on his head.

"Keep your neck warm," his mother warned.

Ben grabbed the big orange wildrag that Fred had given him, wrapped it twice around his neck and knotted it.

Pete left in the old work truck, and Ben rode his four-wheeler down to the shop by the barn and parked it near the pickups. Seth waved him over.

"Hey, Ben, you're helping me today."

"Cool," Ben replied. And he meant it. He liked Seth—his slow drawl, his quick grin, his laid-back ways, and his jokes. Sort of the big brother Ben didn't have.

Seth pointed at Reggie, Alvin, Gabica and Skeeter, working on a big tractor in one bay of the shop. "They're stuck in here, playing mechanic today. You and me get to be outside, building fence."

He backed his truck into another bay. Jumping out and dropping his tailgate with a bang, he hollered, "Come help me load this fencing."

The two of them grabbed reels of barb wire, bundles of steel T-posts, a wire stretcher, a post driver, pliers, hammer, staples, tape measure, string, gloves, a bucket of clips, and a few other odds and ends. As they raced to see who could load more stuff, Ben hardly noticed his neck. The pickup squatted under its heavy load.

"Okay, let's go." Seth gave Ben a slap on the back. They crawled into the cab, puffing from their effort and laughing from the friendly competition.

"You know what?" Ben asked.

"What?" Seth replied.

"I'm kind of glad I'm suspended. I'd rather be outside working with you than in school."

Seth chuckled. "Well, we'll see if you're any better help than those other hon-yocks we left back in the shop."

They didn't have far to drive. Seth pulled up next to a railroad tie brace.

"We already got the corner braces up. Here, grab some

T-posts and head down toward that next brace. Drop one about every 12 feet. Then tie this string to both braces so we can line them up straight."

They worked all morning, driving posts, stretching wire, crimping clips, hammering staples. They talked about Ben's accident and the fight. They compared ideas about school, friends, their dads, and of course—horses.

"I don't know why Dad's so mad. He tells me not to let Derek push me around." Ben handed Seth the post driver.

Seth grunted as he pounded in another post. "Dads have to punish their sons. It's their job." He winked at Ben.

They walked to the next post. "I'd like to see how you handle that colt. We'll have to ride together some time." Seth steadied the post against the string as Ben pounded it in. "Maybe tomorrow afternoon?"

"I hope so. I think Sunday's our last ride. I'll have to see what my dad has lined up for me tomorrow."

The hands on Ben's watch crept slowly toward noon. His stomach growled so loudly that Seth heard it and laughed.

"Okay, okay, let's go get some lunch."

At the ranch driveway, they met the other guys just pulling out. Both pickups stopped and windows rolled down.

"Hey, we're getting sandwiches at the bar. Why don't you guys follow us?"

Seth nodded and waved. He pulled in behind them, and they all headed for Greeley.

The bar was not exactly the typical bar or saloon. It

was the only place in Greeley to get anything to eat or drink. Kids played pool or ping pong, watched TV on the old comfy couches, or sat on the bar stools with their soda or candy. No charge for coffee before 10 A.M. Famous for its Greeley Burgers and Greeley Dogs, the grill busily sizzled and smoked all day long.

The cowboys lined up on bar stools, their twins reflected in the long mirror on the wall behind the bar. Admiring himself, Ben adjusted the brim on his black felt hat.

"Five Greeley Burgers please, with everything on them," Gabica ordered. A swarthy, middle-aged Basque, his nickname was "Basco." Ben didn't even know his first name. "And soda pop for everyone. Put that on the ranch's tab, of course!"

"Where's Alvin?" Seth asked.

"Oh, he's headed up to the Rez," Reggie answered. "His uncle's got a good deal on some horses to maybe buy." The Paiute Indian reservation raised horses and often sold them pretty cheap.

"Bet he can't beat the deal I made up there," Skeeter bragged. "You know how I got that gelding I call Gordon? When he was a scrawny-looking yearling, I traded a good jack knife for him."

Everyone laughed.

"He turned out to be the best horse I ever branded on."

"Well, don't try to brand on that dink paint horse they sold *me* a few years back," Gabica said. "The guy that sold him was as crooked as a dog's hind leg. He told me you could rope on him, so I took him to a branding the next day up at South Fork. First I had to pry his mouth open with a hammer handle to get the bit in. Then he bucked with me when I had a calf headed, jerked my hand down on the horn and broke it. Man, you should've heard that thing go CRACK! I had to wrap it up and keep roping—they didn't have anyone else to help brand."

"That's not the way I heard that story," said Skeeter, twisting his handlebar mustache. His scruffy hat and suspenders gave him an old-timey look, and he always packed a pistol, but he faked a Texas twang, according to Ben's dad. He came from a rich family in New York City, and his name was really Huntley something. "I think you're telling us a 'windy.'"

Hoots and jeers.

"Since we're swapping stories," Skeeter continued, grinning, "I had this horse fall on me once. I thought my foot might be broken, but I kept on working. This cranky old sow I was riding tried to duck out from under me. I forgot about my foot and slapped my spurs into her sides—heard a sound in my foot like a rifle crack. I got the cold sweat, thought I was going to vapor lock, and practically fell off my horse. It wasn't broke, just dislocated, and I had to pop it back into place."

Seth rolled his eyes. "You're full of it, Skeeter! But I've got a true story. My dad used to run mustangs. He and this guy with a little airplane were chasing this herd, flew in low and hit this old lead mare on the head with a tire to try to turn her."

"Oh, yeah, right..." pooh-poohed the others.

"But what was even more exciting was, that knocked the tire off, and they had to land on one tire."

Hoots of disbelieving laughter filled the room.

"Really! That really happened," protested Seth.

"My turn," said Reggie. "That year of the big floods, we were moving some mother cows and little bitty calves across Badger Creek. It was running so high that three calves got sucked through the culvert under the highway and got washed down the creek a ways before we could rope them and pull them out."

"Why, that story's almost believable!" Skeeter said. "Can't you do any better than that?" he teased Reggie.

"Okay...I don't know if any of you have heard this story. A few years back, when I first came to this outfit, two crazy young guys drove a batch of cows through that railroad tunnel just to keep from taking the long way around."

"You're kidding." Gabica shook his head. "What a bunch of yay-hoo's. Who was that?"

"Can't exactly remember." Reggie chuckled and winked.

The Greeley Burgers arrived. Seth drawled, "You guys can keep swapping lies if you want, but I'm going to chow down."

Famished, Ben dug into his burger, wondering about stories and lies. Was telling a "windy" the same as lying? Just how much exaggerating was okay? He had done a little of both.

Ben worked hard the rest of the afternoon. When

Seth dropped him off at his four-wheeler, his head and neck throbbed and the rest of his body ached. At home, he flopped down on the couch to watch TV until dinnertime, but fell asleep.

When the phone rang right after dinner, Ben answered it. Hearing Derek's voice, his anger boiled up, but he quickly jerked to attention. "*What*?...Fire! Dad! At Derek's!"

Chapter 19

Pete grabbed the phone out of his hand. "Derek? Out by the shed? Your folks are out there? Okay, we'll be right there with the truck!"

He slammed the phone down, reaching for his turn-out gear that he kept ready by the door.

"Susie, start the phone chain, then stay off the phone in case someone needs to call you."

Ben already had his hat and jacket on.

"Where do you think you're going?" Pete demanded.

Ben stuttered in surprise, "But...but...I heard you say, 'we.' You said, 'we'll be right there.'"

"I meant me and some of the men," Pete grunted, pulling on his boots.

"I want to fight fire! I want to help!" Ben pleaded. "Remember how I helped at the haystack fire?"

"You're too young. No kids allowed. It's the law."

"Dad, please let me ride along. I'll just watch!"

Pete hesitated and then gave in. "Oh, come on. But you've got to stay out of the way."

"Be careful!" Susie called as they left.

Heart pounding, Ben followed his dad out to the old

pickup. Surging adrenaline banished his aches. They drove to the barn where the fire truck waited and jumped in. It started right up.

"Get out your notes and the manual in case we need them," Pete directed. Ben laid the papers on the seat between them.

The fire truck roared down the valley road, siren screaming. Tonight his dad handled the truck like a pro. Ben couldn't believe they were actually taking the truck to a fire. That nap gave him just the edge he needed.

"Good thing we did some training the other night on the pump panel. I'll run that end of things since I'll be the incident commander. You know how to turn on the pump?" Pete asked.

"Yep," Ben answered.

"Okay, you get that started first thing while I jump out and start pulling down hose. Throw the chock blocks under the back tire. Then get back in the truck. You can watch from there."

Flames engulfed the shed by the time they drove up. With the truck engine running, Ben flipped the toggle switch on the fuel pump and pushed the starter button. The pump howled to life.

He grabbed the heavy triangular chock blocks and jammed one behind the rear wheel and one in front of it. Then he climbed back in the cab. Derek's parents squirted the fire with garden hoses while Derek dragged more hoses from the barn.

Other pickups arrived and men dressed in turn-out

gear ran to help. The truck's spotlights lit up the yard. Over the howling truck, Pete yelled directions into his radio and soon all were working as a team. Ben listened in on the cab radio.

Two men held each hose—one on the nozzle, one behind him bracing his back and taking the weight of the heavy hose. As both hoses bucked and jumped like wild horses, the men struggled to keep their feet.

Ben peered down through the window at his dad, working at the pump panel, and whispered, *Turn down the pressure, Dad!* Ben could see him playing with the levers, and the hoses soon settled down.

Jets of water from one hose squirted the flaming shed, while the other hose protected the nearby house, shop, pump house, and propane tank. Men walked around with shovels, throwing dirt on wind-blown embers and checking for hazards.

Messages crackled across the radio. "Someone shut off the power to this structure...a couple of five-gallon gas cans outside the back wall...I could reach them if I had a pike pole..."

Ben jumped out of the cab, grabbed a pike pole off the fender and handed it to the nearest fire fighter. He could smell the tarry stink of burning creosote from the railroad tie posts. Rivets burst from the metal roof, crackling and popping.

Someone yelled, "I think that roof is going to go! Get back! The whole building is going to collapse!"

Over the roaring fire and howling truck, he heard

something else—the terrified whinnying of horses. He turned toward the sound.

In a nearby set of corrals, several horses raced around in the dark, kicking, bucking, squealing and snorting. He scanned the area—no one seemed to notice them.

Ben glanced at his dad, busy at the pump panel. *Dad said "get in the truck." He didn't actually say "stay in the truck." Hmmm.* He darted toward the corral, hoping his dad hadn't seen him leave.

Once out of the spotlights, Ben stopped to scrutinize the situation. The shop sat between the burning shed and the corrals, but if wind blew sparks or embers this way, things could rapidly get worse. The small stack of hay near the pens could turn deadly in a matter of seconds, Ben knew all too well.

If that happened, not only were the horses in danger, but the fire could spread through the weeds to the barn at the other end of the pens. Even if they didn't get caught in the fire, the horses could injure or kill themselves trying to escape.

I think I'd better try to move those horses. I could put them all out into that big open pen on the other side of the barn. He raced to the barn, threw open the door, and found a light switch. He knew where the halters would be hanging—he'd been here many times.

Carrying a halter and lead rope, he started through the door that led out to the pens and then stopped short. *How am I going to catch a bunch of berserk horses? A bucket of grain? No, crazed horses won't be interested in grain...*

He looked around, spotting a lass rope. He grabbed it and hung the halter back up.

Out in the first pen, he slowly approached the panicked mare. As she ducked and circled him, he calmly organized his coils and built a loop, his eyes never leaving the mare. In his mind he heard Fred's voice: *"Watch her eye, pay attention to her body language."*

He took a few swings, trying to get her attention. An ear flicked toward him. Her feet slowed down almost imperceptibly. *I can see it! I can see what Fred sees!*

With a flick of his wrist, he let the loop fly. Bingo! It dropped softly around her head and settled on her withers. *Wow! That's the best throw I ever made!* He quickly took up the slack, but the mare reared back, squealing, wild-eyed from the sights, sounds and smells.

Ben started to jerk the rope, but stopped. Again he heard Fred: *"You want to keep her calm. Get her to trust you, to be your pardner."*

He slowly and quietly walked up the rope toward her shoulder, gathering his coils. He noticed her hard staring eyes, her tense neck muscles, her feet positioned to kick.

He slowly but confidently reached his hand toward her shoulder. The moment he touched her, he felt her start to relax. He rubbed her and talked soothingly.

"Easy baby, that's a girl, nothing's going to hurt you, easy there, I'm gonna take care of you." As he murmured, he moved the rope up her neck and gently snugged the hondoo, stroking her reassuringly.

She let out her air and lowered her head. Ben felt

the tension leave her neck muscles. The white of her eye disappeared and she seemed to see Ben for the first time. As he turned and walked off confidently, she followed him willingly on a slack rope.

Ben sucked in his breath. He could hardly believe what had just happened. Everything Fred taught him had come to him like second nature. Never had a horse just melted like that for him. She acted like the fire wasn't even there anymore. It looked like magic when Fred did it, but now Ben knew that it wasn't magic at all.

Too bad Fred didn't see that. I think, maybe, he'd be proud of me.

Ben led her through the barn and turned her out the other side into the big pen. Glowing with quiet confidence, he easily caught the other horses and turned them out. They raced down to the far end.

Sneaking back into the truck, Ben watched the fire burn lower, losing its fierceness. Men doused hot spots and used fire axes to break apart the burning railroad ties. He knew their greasy creosote could smolder for hours, maybe restarting the fire in the night.

Watching the men clean up the scene, Ben thought about catching the horses. He relived each moment, savoring the pleasure of his growing confidence and skill. Suddenly his daydream took a big detour, interrupted by a rude thought.

Sunday—that's day after tomorrow! Dad says I'm going to buck out those colts Sunday. He wilted inside. *Why do I have to prove I'm tough? Why is it so hard to please Dad?*

Feelings about Soapsuds and Black Bob swirled around in his mind, blending into his feelings about the horses tonight. How they softened when he handled them. How they looked at him with trusting brown eyes. Would the two colts feel like that when he bucked them out? Would they look at him like that afterwards?

I don't think so.

He knew how they would look. Just like that sorrel colt looked after his dad finished with him a few weeks ago. Defeated—not like a "pardner."

He took a long deep breath. *I won't do that to them... but how will I tell him?*

He rubbed the fog off the window, looking for his dad. *It's like this window is between us. He's on one side, I'm on the other, and there's this fog. He just doesn't hear me.*

Chapter 20

When they got home, Pete and Ben told Susie all about the fire.

Susie said, "I talked to Derek's mom on the phone. She took him to Elko to the doctor this morning. He was complaining about his back, and he thought you broke his nose. I guess nothing was wrong with him though."

Ben snorted. "I saw him dragging hoses around tonight. Nothing's wrong with his back. He's such a faker."

Saturday morning, Ben helped his dad work on their pickup. They changed oil and put on new brake pads. Hoping he'd have time to ride with Seth, Ben asked his dad as they were cleaning up for lunch, "Will you be needing me after lunch, Dad?"

"You bet!" Pete answered with a grin, rubbing his knuckles playfully on Ben's head. "You're my right-hand man!"

Ben grinned and ducked away, but inside he grumbled. Usually he loved helping his dad, but this afternoon...well, he had his own plans.

"We need to go check those cows out on the Murphy place. Make sure they got enough feed and water, make sure gates are closed and no fences are down. See if any of them need doctoring."

Ben brightened. It sounded like they'd be riding.

"You take that gray colt of Fred's you've been riding."

Ben's heart lurched. He'd get to ride Soapsuds with his dad! But, his dad called him "that colt of Fred's."

Of course, he *did* belong to Fred. Only, in Ben's mind, Soapsuds rightfully belonged to *him*. They had bred and raised him—had Pete forgotten? Couldn't his dad see that Soapsuds would always be Ben's horse, in a way?

No, of course he couldn't see that. Ben sighed deeply.

"Oh, and Ben...I've been going to tell you...that kid's saddle of yours is way too small for you. You need a good A-fork saddle that fits you now. You can have that oldest one of mine." He slapped Ben on the back. "You'll need a good seat when you buck out those colts."

Ben tried to smile but said nothing.

After lunch they hitched up the gooseneck trailer and then caught and saddled the horses and loaded them. The Murphy field, fifteen miles by road, was a small neighboring place bought up by the Circle A some years back in a small neighboring valley. The herd they were checking had been trailed down the mountain a month or so ago and dumped in the alfalfa field to eat stubble.

They talked about Derek as they drove.

"You know, Ben, you hang out with him too much."

"But there's only Derek and James that are my age..."

"Derek's a liar, got no sense of responsibility." Pete glanced over at Ben. "He's not like you." He paused. "I know there's not a lot of kids your age. Just be your own man."

A warm glow filled Ben's chest. His dad had just paid him a back-handed compliment, but it wasn't exactly true. He frowned, twisting his mouth to one side.

"Dad, sometimes it's...hard to tell the truth when you think maybe you'll get in trouble. Sometimes it's easier to just...fudge a little on the truth. You hope no one notices..." His voice trailed off.

Pete said quietly, "Yeah, I know what you mean."

"You do?" Ben stared at his dad in disbelief.

"Hey, there's not a man alive that has never told a lie. I admit I've told my share. But a real man tells the truth. The Bible says it's better to be a poor man that tells the truth than a rich man that's a liar."

Ben chewed on that. He didn't like it when other people lied. He thought about his own little lies lately.

I want to be a real man. No more lies for me, not even little ones.

The rutted dirt track kept their loaded rig at a crawl. They wound through hills, crossed the railroad tracks, dropped into ravines, and climbed little slopes. After an hour of driving, they'd only gone about ten miles. Pete turned on the radio, singing along with the songs he knew.

Ben wanted to announce his decision about the colts but he knew his dad would throw a fit. He especially wanted to do a good job starting them because one of them might become his next colt. Not that any other colt could ever fill the hole in his heart that Soapsuds had left.

Nervously twiddling his thumbs, he stalled for time, staring out the side window. He dreamed about the ranch that he would run someday, or maybe even own. Sagebrush, hay, cattle, and horses—the lifeblood of ranching.

Only weeks ago, Ben, Pete, and Fred rode cleanup, driving the last of the herd down the mountain to the home ranch. The Circle A, like other ranches in the area, ran their cattle on the mountains from spring through fall.

The mountains were public land—land belonging to the American people and run by government agencies. The lower sections were administered by the BLM—the Bureau of Land Management. The higher parts of the mountains were U.S. Forest Service. Each rancher was assigned a certain area, called an allotment.

Ranchers carefully maintained the grazing land so they could make a living from year to year. Ben knew that grazing controlled the dry grass and brush that could fuel a lightning fire. Fires were hard to fight in these remote, roadless mountains where no one lived, and many a rancher had lost much or all of his yearly grazing to wildfires.

Good thing we've got that truck now, Ben thought. *Maybe we won't have as many bad fires.*

In this dry barren country, it took a lot of land to run cattle, much more land than most ranchers could afford to buy. The cattle scrounged about for what grass they could find among the sagebrush, turning it into food for humans.

The allotment system meant that Pete and the other buckaroos spent a lot of time moving cattle. As soon as the new spring grass carpeted the mountain slopes, they trailed them up from the home ranch where they'd been eating hay all winter. Mother cows still nursed calves born a couple of months earlier. The buckaroos branded the new crop of calves and then moved the herd to the Circle A's BLM allotment.

Later they were trailed up into the mountains, on their Forest Service allotment, where they spent the rest of the summer. They had to be moved off the forest by a certain date in fall. Back on the home ranch, they grazed off the stubble left on all the hay fields. When no more stubble remained, it was time to start feeding them hay for the rest of the winter. In spring the cycle started all over again.

Ben looked at the endless waves of sage. *Too bad cattle don't eat sagebrush. We'd never run out of feed. We wouldn't have to feed hay all winter.*

But they did have to feed all winter. During the long hot days of summer, the buckaroos grew and harvested hay. They irrigated the alfalfa fields and then cut the alfalfa with a swather—a gigantic tractor lawnmower. After drying a few days, they turned the swaths with a huge rotating rake pulled by a tractor.

In a few days, when the moisture content was just right, a baler picked up the swaths of cut alfalfa and packed them into bales. Harobeds picked up the bales and stacked them. Working a-horseback every day is a buckaroo's dream, but farming must be done. Ben had started haying several years ago, driving a rake and a swather during summer vacation. Recently, as his driving skills had improved and he'd grown taller, he'd even learned to drive a harobed.

In the fall, the buckaroos drove the bulls, the mother cows, and the half-grown calves home before the winter snows trapped them on the mountain. After the fall cattle drive, cowboys branded any calves that were missed in the spring. Then they were weaned, sold, and trucked to California to be fattened on grass before butchering. After eating the stubble off the hay fields, the cattle would be fed baled hay for the rest of the winter—hay that had been produced that summer. This was ranch life—the life Ben knew and loved.

Ben finally turned away from the window, working up his nerve. "Dad?" His voice cracked and he cleared his throat. "Dad, about those colts tomorrow..."

Pete gave him a sideways glance.

Ben gulped. *I guess there's only one way to do this. Like jumping into cold water. Just do it.*

"Dad, I'm not going to buck out those colts."

There. Relief flooded him. He'd stood up to his dad. He'd been his own man, just like his dad had said.

At the same time, he felt fear. *What now?* He stole a look at his dad.

"You *what?*"

Pete stared at Ben with an astonished expression.

Ben plowed ahead boldly. "That's not the way I want to start a colt. I want him to trust me, to be my pardner."

"Oh, here we go again," Pete said, annoyed. "*Fred* this and *Fred* that. Yes, you are going to do as I say!"

Ben tightened his lips. He took a deep breath. "Dad,

I'm not a little kid. I'm twelve years old, almost a man."

He paused and then added in his most manly voice, "You said to be my own man." Another pause. He held his head higher. "I have my own ideas about horses."

Pete's eyebrows shot up. He looked hard at Ben, opened his mouth, closed it, and turned his face quickly toward his side window.

Ben looked out the window too, but saw nothing unusual out there. He wondered what caught his dad's attention.

Suddenly the truck jerked hard to the right, slamming to a teeth-jarring stop and throwing Pete and Ben forward against their seat belts. Horses whinnied. Iron-shod hooves clattered in the trailer behind them.

Chapter 21

"What in tarnation?" Pete turned off the key and jumped out to see what had happened. He looked down under the front bumper.

"I'll be a dirty rotten son-of-a-gun," he said disgustedly, jamming his hands onto his hips. "A broken tie rod."

The broken metal rod had jammed into the ground, bringing the rig to a rude, jolting stop.

"Can you fix it?" Ben asked.

"No. We'll have to leave our rig here and ride out. I'll get someone to tow the trailer home and haul the truck."

"Well, I'm getting a drink before we go." Ben zipped up his jacket and helped himself to the water jug they always carried.

Pete poured a quick thermos cup of coffee. "Get those horses unloaded while I drink this," he said.

Ben opened the trailer tailgate and unloaded Soapsuds, tying him to the side of the trailer. He opened the divider and hooked it with a clang.

"Hey, Dad!" he called. "Come look at Hoagie!"

Pete put down his cup and joined Ben inside the trailer.

A cut above Hoagie's left hind hoof left blood pooling on the floor. Blood ran down his face from an ugly gash above his eye. Pete gently stroked the horse as he checked him out.

He pointed to blood on the divider. "Looks like he scrambled to keep his feet, and hit his head here," pointing to the front end of the trailer. "Darn it."

He rubbed his chin. "Well, I guess you'd better stay here with him while I ride home and get help."

Dad's going to ride Soapsuds home? Ben did some quick thinking.

"Dad, wait. I've got a better idea. You're good at doctoring, and I don't have any experience. And I know Soapsuds better than you. Let me ride home while you do the doctoring."

Pete frowned. "I can get along with your colt just fine. And I'm sure I can get home faster than you could."

"Dad! You don't trust me to do a man's job, do you? You want me to prove I'm tough enough, but now you're treating me like a kid!"

"What? I've never said anything about proving anything!"

"But that's what you think about me, isn't it? I heard what you said to Mom that night..."

Pete's face turned red. "You *what?*"

Ben immediately realized his mistake. He began to stutter, his voice cracking. "Oops...I mean...I didn't...well, yes, I did eavesdrop by the window...I'm sorry, Dad...I know it was wrong...but I can be as tough as you! I can do it, Dad! Please!"

Pete didn't look at Ben or answer. He opened the hatch to the gooseneck and got out the emergency vet kit. Ben hardly dared to breathe as Pete rummaged through the bandages, bottles, ointments, and syringes.

"Don't run him. Keep him to a trot, and walk him plenty. Remember he's just a colt." He didn't look up. "Figure on several hours of riding—it's hard to say. Stay on the road so you don't get lost."

Ben's heart beat faster. "Dad, I can get there in half that time. I know some shortcuts..."

Pete cut him off. "No!"

He looked Ben in the eye. "I know you want to prove you've got guts. But this is not the time. It's cold and windy, it could snow, and it might get dark before you get home."

"I won't have trouble with him, Dad. He'll go wherever I ask him to go."

"Ben, I've seen how that horse can buck."

He's actually worried about me. Ben tried not to smile.

"Just stay on the road. I know it's the long way, but...I don't want anything to happen to you, and...I'm depending on you, pardner. Better be safe than sorry."

Ben sighed. "Okay, Dad. You can count on me."

He pulled on his chaps, buckled on his spurs, tightened the cinch, and then put the snaffle on Soapsuds.

"See you soon," he said confidently, swinging up into the saddle.

Adrenaline surged through his body as he legged Soapsuds into a smooth jog trot. He followed the colt's rhythm, posting up and down, letting the powerful hindquarters push him slightly out of the saddle with every other stride.

Following the dirt road up a hump, he stopped at the top and turned in the saddle. His dad, watching him, waved. Ben waved back and trotted down the other side, out of sight.

We're on our own now.

He wondered what his dad might be thinking.

I thought he wanted me to be tough. He didn't care if I got bucked off or hurt. I can't believe that now he wants me to play it safe. I don't get it.

The narrow dirt road wound between tall sagebrush, around rocks, and over dry creek beds. Being on his own usually filled Ben with excitement, but this felt different.

So far to go before dark. Dull gray clouds threatening snow. So much depending on his horse.

He remembered all the things that had gone wrong with the colt: how Soapsuds shied that night in the corral, how he could spin, how he could buck, how he could scatter on the trail when something spooked him. How most of that had been Ben's own fault.

Dad said, be tough enough to get back on if you're out by yourself and something happens. Might something happen? If it did, could I?

He pictured himself lying there in the freezing cold, with a broken leg, hoping someone would find him.

A voice in his head asked: *Would Soapsuds stay with you if you came off? Or would he head home, the empty saddle announcing that his rider was in need of help?*

Fear crept in around the edges of his stomach. Ben felt the colt tensing up under him, ready to spook at the slightest thing. He shied at a big dark rock.

Ben took a deep breath, and heard another little voice: *Remember everything Fred taught you—about riding, about trusting your horse.*

Whenever the colt started acting spooky, Ben zigzagged him around the sagebrush, keeping him too busy to think about mischief.

As he forced himself to relax and trust Soapsuds, the colt relaxed, and Ben's breathing evened out. *Clop-clop-clop-clop.* Like the ticking of a clock, the even cadence of trotting hooves marked the slow passing of time.

"This saddle is great," he told Soapsuds. Talking out loud to the colt helped ease his anxiety. "It just fits my butt, almost like it was made just for me. Do you like it too? Dad says it has fit every horse he ever put it on."

Comfortable and roomy, it put him so close to Soapsuds, his legs just draped around the colt's sides. He could feel the flex of every muscle, almost like he was bareback. He felt like he could stick to that saddle even if Soapsuds turned a somersault in mid-air.

Time dragged as the miles ahead seemed to get no shorter. They cut some of the curves, to save time. Even when taking a shortcut, Ben could always see the road nearby.

He remembered long rides he'd been on with his dad. Moving cows kept your mind occupied. Doing a job kept your horse's mind occupied. Today, alone, with no cows to follow, only his drifting thoughts kept him company.

"Hey, Soapsuds, you know tomorrow's my last day to ride you."

He caught his breath at the thought and squeezed his eyes shut, willing the tears to go away. His strong love for Soapsuds, mixed with happiness and sadness, ached inside his chest.

"When Fred starts riding you, will you forget all about me? Huh, boy?"

Ben groaned, running his hand under the colt's thick mane. Why couldn't he just ride Soapsuds the rest of his life?

"Surely if Fred was going to give you back to me, he'd have told me."

Soapsuds stepped on a sharp rock, stumbling. He limped for a few strides before he found his rhythm again. Slowing the colt to a walk, Ben gave him a breather.

He thought back over the last weeks, searching his memory for anything Fred might have said or done that could have been a hint. A hint Ben might have missed.

"That colt of yours." Yes! *I knew he'd said something, but did he really mean it?*

Ben could think of nothing else to feed his slim hope. He thought about begging Fred. *No, that would never do.*

Maybe his dad would consider breeding old Whitey one more time and getting another colt out of her. But it wouldn't be the same.

"I could never find another colt like you," he told

Soapsuds. "Not if I had all the money in the world. And I don't even have any money anyhow."

Money.

"That's it! I'll buy you back! I wonder how much money I could make next summer?"

It might take a couple years to make enough money. And what if Fred refused to sell him?

"If we lived back in the old days, we could just run away from home. We'd roam the West, riding with the vaqueros, driving longhorns. We'd be the envy of everyone who saw us. They'd all try to buy you, but I wouldn't sell you for any amount of money. We'd be famous..."

He spied a torn sack with trash. *Sheesh! It's even out here!* Then before he could dodge the plastic bottle underfoot...CRACKLE!

The colt sprang into the air. Ben's heart leaped into his mouth. Grabbing his rope, he clamped his elbow to his side.

Relax!

Soapsuds hit the ground. He walked off as if nothing had happened.

Ben let out his breath and gave a shaky laugh. He reached up and gratefully rubbed the colt's warm neck.

He talked out loud to calm himself. "Man, if I wasn't daydreaming, I'd have seen that coming. I've got to pay attention. Next time I might not be so lucky."

But he'd stuck to the saddle like glue without even trying, like a hand in a glove. And the colt moved like a cloud, light and smooth.

I wish I had it on video so I could watch it over and over!

Approaching the railroad track, Ben considered the possibility of following it instead of the winding dirt road. He knew where the tracks passed near the ranch. It was a much more direct route, and would be quite a shortcut. The only trouble was, it tunneled through a steep jagged rocky mountain that he'd have to find a way around. He didn't know that area.

Reggie talked about some crazy guys that drove cows through the tunnel. *Hmm. Riding through the tunnel would save LOTS of time!*

But...could he? It sounded scary. He had promised to stay on the road, and his dad would kill him if he knew.

Well, he doesn't need to know. If I don't tell him, I haven't really lied.

But what if Soapsuds panicked or acted up in there? It could be bad footing in the dark tunnel. What if he got his foot caught? What if a train came?

Ben jumped as the train in his imagination came to life with a sharp whistle. The ground rumbled. Soon the train appeared around a bend.

Another train would not come for some time. He pretty much knew the schedule—*if* they stuck to it—and there were never two trains right in a row. He must decide quickly. Sweat broke out all over his body.

Chapter 22

Ben looked at his watch. If he stayed on the road, he'd be riding home in the dark. He dared not push the colt any harder. He loved him too much to take that chance.

But what about taking a chance in the tunnel? Those other guys had made it okay, and it would shorten the trip. That would be better for the colt, Ben reasoned. His dad and Hoagie would get help quicker.

Ben steadied the colt as the train roared past, turning him tightly around some sagebrush. Then, before he could talk himself out of it, he reined Soapsuds toward the track. It was still a ways to the tunnel. They must hurry.

"Okay, you've had a long walk and plenty of time to rest. Let's go now!" He pushed the colt into a brisk trot. "You can rest again at the tunnel."

After a good twenty minutes of long-trotting, the entrance to the tunnel loomed in front of them. Ben reined the colt to a stop and eyeballed the situation. He estimated it could be a hundred yards to the circle of light at the other end—the length of a football field. He heard the colt's heavy blowing and felt his ribs move in and out, in and out, as his breath made frosty clouds in front of them.

"Let's do it!" Ben's scalp tingled as he guided the colt into the dark tunnel.

Soapsuds stepped uncertainly between the track and the wall on the left. With each breath, soft snorts fluttered through his nostrils. He stretched his neck downward, exploring where to put his feet.

Why didn't I think to grab that flashlight from the pickup? Oh well, Dad might need it.

The colt froze and sucked back a little. Ben sniffed. It smelled like something dead, but he couldn't make out anything in the dark. He flapped his stirrups against the colt's sides.

"What's the matter? Got a hitch in your git-along? Come on!" Soapsuds didn't want to be hurried, so Ben let him pick his way.

Like an optical illusion, the other end of the tunnel appeared farther away than when they entered. *Maybe we should go faster. Just in case a train comes. What if they don't stick to their usual schedule today?*

He strained his ears for the rumble of an oncoming train or a warning whistle. But he only heard the whistling wind over the echoing clop of hooves. He swallowed hard, sucking in deep breaths. *How could 100 yards be this far?*

Suddenly a dreadful thought occurred to him. *What if that story Reggie told about the tunnel was just a windy? Maybe it never really happened!* Nausea clutched at his stomach.

Even though Ben shivered in the freezing wind, nervous sweat broke out on his body. The whole tunnel idea seemed so stupid now. If anything went wrong, how would he ever explain this to his dad? *If* he even made it out alive. A dizzying fear threatened to paralyze his brain. He focused on the cl-clop, cl-clop of the colt's steady walk.

He prayed out loud, trying to calm himself. "Dear God, I know I shouldn't be in here. I'm sorry I didn't listen to my dad. But here I am. Please get us out of here safely."

He took a better hold on his reins, just in case. The colt threw his head up and down, so Ben shortened his reins even more. The colt jigged and snorted. The tighter Ben held on, the more the colt tensed up.

Fred says I need to trust my horse, so he can trust me.

Uncertainly, he fed out a little more rein, and felt the colt immediately start to relax. The light at the end of the tunnel got closer and closer. Ben started to relax too. His confidence increasing, he gave the colt even more rein.

As they emerged from the tunnel, Ben let out a long breath and laughed shakily.

Stopping the colt, he dropped his reins, leaned forward and hugged him, rubbing both sides of his neck hard through the thick, damp, warm hair.

"Hey, pardner! We made it! It won't be long now 'til we're home!" He lay on the colt's neck, breathing in the good smell of horse sweat. Soapsuds dropped his head to the ground, letting out a big sigh and grabbing a few bites of dry grass.

Suddenly a distant whistle made the hairs on the back of Ben's neck stand up. The ground began to shake and so did Ben. Feeling dizzy, he turned Soapsuds and trotted him quickly away from the tracks, as far as they could get. When the train passed, Ben jumped off his horse and vomited. He leaned on the warm colt, sweating and shaking.

"Where did *that* train come from? So much for their schedule. I will *never* disobey Dad again," he promised Soapsuds. As the freezing wind blew a flurry of popcorn snow all over Ben, he stood up and checked his watch. The little pellets, pointed on one side, bounced like hail.

"Dad's waiting, we've got to hustle!" he told the colt, getting back on and trotting him back to the tracks. "We've got to get home while we can still see. Man, how did those clouds get so dark so fast?" Since he left the road and passed the tunnel, he didn't know exactly where he was. He tried not to think about that.

Soon the tracks, the ground, and the sagebrush blurred under a thin skiff of snow. *Boy, am I glad I put my wildrag on before we left.* He snugged it higher on his neck.

Ben kept his eyes peeled for the familiar dirt road that crossed the tracks above the ranch. He knew the way on his four-wheeler, coming from home. But they had already passed several dirt road crossings. He hoped he'd recognize the right one. By now a good inch of snow made everything look the same. He guessed his road could be maybe two miles from the tunnel. Just a wild guess—he'd never been this way before.

"Man, it's getting cold," Ben said, nervously talking to himself. The longer they rode, the more his neck bothered him, but he tried not to think about it. "Sure glad I've got gloves. I hope it doesn't snow much more—I've got to spot that road. How you doin'? You hanging in there okay?"

He slowed Soapsuds to a walk and then a stop. "Look here. What do you think? Is this it?"

Ben studied a narrow road through the sagebrush. Usually he could see Horse Canyon if he looked up toward the mountains, but a murky gray curtain of snow hid the landmarks today. He looked at the lay of the land—did it feel familiar?

Slowly he said, "I think this is it...yeah, this must be it... come on, let's go home."

They left the tracks behind and started down the road at a walk. What if it wasn't the right road? Wherever it came out, Ben thought he could probably figure out their location and get home eventually. He knew most of the roads around the ranch for several miles in any direction— when they weren't disguised by too much snow.

The only problem: if anything "happened," as his dad said, no one knew where to look for them. If they had stayed on the main road, at least they stood a chance of someone coming by.

But nothing would go wrong. Ben trusted his horse, and his horse trusted him. They were partners.

He kept his eyes peeled for a dry creek bed to appear alongside the road...if this was the right road. Horse Creek—dry this time of year—drained out of Horse Canyon, passed under the tracks through a culvert farther up ahead, and ran alongside the road for a bit.

"There it is!" Ben sucked in a huge breath and let it

out, grinning. *Thank you, God.* With the snow and darkness creeping in early, they'd barely be able to see to get home.

"Come on, boy, let's go!" shouted Ben in excitement. They hit a high trot for about a mile, while they could still see well and then dropped back to a fast walk for the last stretch. Even though Ben could hardly wait to get home, he didn't want the colt to come in too sweaty. But when he saw Fred and Seth at the barn, filling the hay feeders in the corral under the big yard light, he broke Soapsuds into a quick lope, yelling at the top of his voice.

"Fred! Seth!"

He could see the look of shock on their faces as they turned to see him jump off his horse.

"Ben! What are you doing here? Where's Pete? What's happened?"

"Dad's broke down on the road out to the Murphy place! And Hoagie's hurt!"

Fred calmly took charge of the situation. "Seth, you finish chores and take care of that colt of his. Tell Susie what's going on. Ben and I will go get Pete and Hoagie. Are you okay, Ben?"

"I'm fine," Ben shouted. "Come on, Dad needs help!" But in the back of his mind, he filed away those words: *"that colt of his."*

Fred jumped in his truck and backed up to one of the trailers parked by the barn. Ben handed his McCarty to Seth, giving Soapsuds a hug around the neck and tenderly rubbing his face.

"Thanks," he whispered to the colt. "See you later."

He hurried off to help Fred hitch up the trailer. In a few minutes they were on the road.

Ben cranked the heater up and turned the fan on high so air blasted out at him. "I'm frozen," he said, shivering. It felt so good to sink into the soft pickup seat. He rubbed his hands together in front of the heater vent and then rubbed his cheeks and nose.

"I'll bet," Fred replied, and pointed to the thermos. "Help yourself."

Ben poured himself a cup of steaming coffee. He shuddered as he sipped the bitter liquid, but it warmed his insides. "At least Dad's got coffee and water," he said.

"How far out is he?" Fred asked.

"Oh, ten miles or more. You know...past that big dip by those rocky pinnacles."

Fred grunted. "You're lucky you got back by dark, with the snow. Although it seems to have quit now. How'd you get back so quick?"

Ben hesitated, biting his lip. He wanted to tell Fred how the colt came through for him. How could he do that without admitting they went through the tunnel?

"Well, we went...we took a...shortcut. Please don't tell Dad! He told me to stay on the road and...and I said I would."

He sent Fred a pleading look. Not answering, Fred ran his tongue over his teeth.

But Ben couldn't keep from bragging. "Soapsuds might not step in a hot bear track for me, but...he'll go through a dark tunnel!"

"The *tunnel?*" Fred said in disbelief. "You went through the *tunnel?* What a fool thing to do."

"But Fred! Reggie told that story yesterday about the guys that drove some cows through the tunnel. If they could do it, I could do it too. And it was important to hurry. My dad needed help. You told me to trust my horse, and I did!" He decided it might be better not to tell what happened afterwards.

Fred chuckled, turning to stare at Ben, but saying nothing. Ben wondered what was so funny about it.

"Here!" Ben said, pointing. "Turn here."

"I know how to get to the Murphy place!" Fred said sarcastically. "I've been there a jillion times."

"Oh, yeah, sorry. I didn't mean to be telling you what to do." Ben grinned apologetically. The empty trailer rattled behind them as they hit the bumpy dirt road.

Now that the truth was out, they talked about Soapsuds and how he did today. Fred nodded as Ben explained that he tried to keep the colt from getting too stressed on the long ride.

"I *did* worry a little today because of...some things that happened a few weeks ago...that I haven't told you about. I wasn't sure I could trust Soapsuds, or that he really trusted me either."

Ben filled him in—how he came off Soapsuds in the pen, and how the colt spun out from under him in the sagebrush when he hadn't been paying attention. It felt good not to be hiding lies anymore.

"I knew all that," Fred said with a grin.

"You *what*? How could you know that?" Ben's eyes bugged out.

"The night at the pen, I heard your four-wheeler and stepped out my door to see who was driving around. I watched you by the moonlight."

Ben hung his head. "I'm sorry. It was a stupid thing to do."

"And that hooey about playing too rough at school... Face it, kid, you're just not a very good liar. Your face and your tone of voice give you away."

Ben didn't say anything for a minute. Then he replied slowly, "Well, I've learned my lesson—about lying, I mean. My dad says a real man tells the truth."

"Your dad's a good man. He and I don't see eye to eye on everything, but he's a man of his word."

Ben sighed. "He and I don't see eye to eye on everything, either. Especially horses."

"I know. Hey, kid, I'm turning that colt out tomorrow."

"Tomorrow?" The word chilled Ben.

"You did a good job with him. Now we'll just let him grow up a bit more."

A compliment from Fred? "Thanks! And thanks for taking the time to teach me."

But even as he spoke the words, the hair on Ben's neck prickled. *"We'll* just let him?" What did Fred mean by that?

And Fred's words to Seth: *"that colt of his."* Was Fred trying to tell him something? Would Fred really give him back his colt? Had Ben proved he was worthy?

Chapter 23

"Tomorrow." Ben cringed at the dreaded word. Tomorrow might be his last chance to ever ride Soapsuds—unless Fred gave him back to Ben.

"Hey, Fred, can I just get him out one last time and check him over? Just saddle him up and see how he feels, after today?" Ben hoped Fred would okay one last ride. "Not that he needs riding," he added quickly. "He might be pretty sore."

Fred nodded. "Sure, kid. I know you want to tell him goodbye."

Ben stared at Fred. *Goodbye?* The bottom dropped out of his stomach.

I thought sure Fred had been hinting all this time. Of course he knows how I feel about the colt. Doesn't he? Isn't that why he asked me to help him in the first place?

Turning his face to his window, Ben gulped back tears. There was nothing else to say. Silence filled the truck on the long ride down the bumpy road. Just as well—Ben was too tired to talk.

Ben remembered their pickup ride together, a few weeks back, and their talk—about Soapsuds and other things. That day he and Fred forged a friendship. Now Fred had become more than just a friend. Ben idolized him, along with his dad—two men that someday he wanted to be like.

Finally a truck and trailer appeared in their headlights.

"Hey, there's my dad!" called Ben excitedly, pointing.

Fred brought the rattling rig to a halt, let Ben out, and drove on ahead to find a place to turn around. Ben ran to his dad, and they hugged each other.

"You made it, pardner!" Pete slapped Ben on the back.

Ben laughed. "You didn't think I would?"

Pete grinned. "Well, I admit I worried. But all I could do was sit here and wait."

When Fred drove up, they quickly loaded Hoagie, climbed in the truck and headed for home. Removing his gloves, Pete rubbed his hands in front of the heater. "Ahhh!"

Ben sat in the middle. "I was worried about you, Dad."

"Well, it was hard to sit there and do nothing, wondering if you were okay or in trouble, with the snow and all, just trusting and praying that you were man enough to handle it."

Ben pondered that for a moment. "I got kind of scared, so I guess I'm not as brave as I thought."

Pete snorted. "Nothing wrong with being scared. Being a man is when you get the job done even though you're scared. You did good all right, Ben."

Ben grinned and looked down, glowing inside.

"Did that colt handle okay?"

"He was *great*, Dad! You should've seen him."

"You made good time. You didn't run him, did you?"

"No." *Hmm, what should I say?* Ben thought. *I've got to think of a good explanation. Or, I could just tell him the truth. No more lies.*

Fred's elbow dug into his side. "Uh, well, we didn't exactly stay on the road..."

"You didn't?" Pete's voice rose.

"We...uh...we took a short cut...we...uh..." Ben heaved a big sigh. Then in a small voice he admitted, "We went through the tunnel."

Speaking faster, he added, "I was so worried about you, Dad. I had to get back as quick as I could! And I'd heard about some guys that had done it, so I figured I could do it too." There. The truth was out. He braced himself.

Pete started to explode, but caught his words and swallowed them. He clenched his jaw and said, "What's done is done."

Fred leaned toward Ben and asked, in a sneaky tone of voice, "You know who the guys were?"

"No. Who?"

Pete shot Fred a warning glare.

Fred returned an evil grin to Pete and said, "Well, one of 'em was your dad. Hee-hee-hee!"

"I thought I told you not to tell him that story about me," Pete retorted angrily.

Fred cackled. "I didn't. He heard it from Reggie."

Pete squeezed his lips together hard and then gave a loud annoyed sigh.

"He's just like his dad, ain't he?" Fred peered over at Pete. "He can be a hothead, but he's his own man. And he gets the job done."

Ben noticed that Fred had said he was "his own man." *Why did he say that? He can't know that Dad told me that very thing today!* He remembered all the other times Fred seemed to know what he was thinking. *How does he know stuff? Is he really a mind reader?*

Pete licked his bottom lip, considering. "Yeah," he finally said with a proud smile. "He's a lot like his old man."

Ben looked straight ahead. He didn't know what to say. The way they were talking about him made him feel awkward, but happy. *I think they're saying they're both proud of me, but no one's exactly saying it. That's okay.*

"Dad, I'm sorry I disobeyed you and went through the tunnel. You know, I almost lied about it, but...well, remember that talk we just had?"

Pete reached over, jerked Ben's hat off, and roughly but affectionately rubbed his knuckles around on his head. "Yeah, I remember."

Ben ducked his head. "Ouch!" But he grinned at his dad. His dad's blue eyes laughed back at him as he crammed Ben's hat back on his head.

"Hey. You're tougher than I thought you were. You did good today. And you stood up to your old man and said what you thought about the colts."

Ben swelled up inside. He felt like he might burst.

"You know, Ben," continued Pete, "I had a lot of time today to think about you and that colt. I'm proud of the job you've done with him. Fred has even bragged on you."

Embarrassed, Fred drawled, "Well, I'm just showing him that there's more than one way to start a colt."

Pete nodded. "You know, I've been thinking, Fred's ideas have some merit. Ben, I'm going to let you start those colts any way you want to. You earned that privilege today. So tomorrow, you show me what you've got."

Ben couldn't believe his ears. He grinned so hard, it almost hurt.

Wow, Dad admitted that Fred's way is good too. And Fred agreed that there's more than just his way.

"Thanks, Dad! And thanks, Fred!"

A huge yawn threatened to split his face in two. He took off his hat and leaned his head on his dad's shoulder. He hadn't told them about the last train, but maybe that story could wait until later—until some day when they were all telling windies.

Waking up as they pulled into the yard, his empty stomach rumbled fiercely.

Susie's cooking had never tasted as good as it did that evening in the warm cozy kitchen. She even gave them seconds on dessert.

"Suz, you've outdone yourself!" She pretended to duck away as Pete gave her a pat on the behind.

I don't think I'm even going to call Derek, Ben thought as he finished eating.

But later that evening, the phone rang. Ben knew who it would be. *I'll just tell him I'm not doing it tomorrow... oops, that's a lie...what should I tell him?*

"Hello?"

Derek's voice sounded awkward. "Hey, Ben...hey, I owe you a big apology. I'm really sorry, man. I mean it." Derek paused. "I hope we can still be friends."

Ben's eyebrows shot up. That's not what he'd expected to hear. He stammered, "I...well...hey, thanks...that's okay."

"Hey, Ben, you gonna buck out those colts tomorrow?"

Ben stammered again, "Uh...maybe...uh, well...you wanna come watch me start them?"

"Sure. What time?"

"Right after lunch. We've got church in the morning."

"Okay, see you then, buddy."

Ben hung up, his eyes big with surprise. Surprise that Derek had apologized. Surprise that he'd told Derek he could come. Surprise that he wasn't very mad at Derek anymore. Maybe Derek wasn't such a bad guy after all.

I wonder what he'll think of my way of starting the colts.

And, surprised at his own self-confidence, Ben realized he didn't even care. *Derek won't get it. But it doesn't matter.*

After lunch on Sunday, Ben hurried out to catch Soapsuds. He brushed him down, running his hands over the colt's legs, feeling for any puffiness. He appeared to be sound, and showed no signs of limping. Ben saddled and bridled him and rode him quietly past the corral where the two colts waited.

Derek had lost his back-road driving privileges in the old truck, so his dad dropped him off and visited a minute with Pete and Fred before he left. Ben rode up and joined the little group.

"Hey," Derek said, "thanks for moving those horses the other night. Dad saw you but didn't have a chance to talk to you. He says he couldn't believe how you caught them. It almost looked like magic."

Ben glanced at his dad. *Oh boy, now he finds out I didn't stay in the truck. I'm going to get it now.*

Pete looked sideways at Ben, frowning, looking like he was deciding something. A smile played around the corners of his mouth, but he said nothing. Ben relaxed. He noticed Fred watching him, pride written all over his face.

Pete grinned and said, "Fred, you look as pleased as a fox eating yellow jackets."

Fred teased, "Sounds like my star pupil has been showing off."

"My dad says I ought to hang out with you more," Derek continued. "He says you're a good influence on me." He laughed. Again Ben and Pete exchanged glances, eyebrows raised. Pete gave Ben a little nod.

Derek ran his hand across the colt's rump, scratching him affectionately. "You didn't brush his tail very good," he said. "He's got some orange baling twine caught in it."

He gave it a jerk. But it wasn't hanging loose at all.

Soapsuds's head flew up and Ben felt him start to wad up. He automatically relaxed into the saddle, reaching for the Cheyenne roll, as the colt ran backwards, bogged his head, and exploded into one huge buck. When Soapsuds landed with Ben still astride, they just walked off like nothing had happened.

"Yee-haw!" shouted Pete. "Did you see how high his

feet came off the ground? Just like that first time you saddled him!"

"Naw!" protested Ben. "He just took a little hop."

"The heck he did! I could see right under his belly!" Fred said. "It just felt easy because you rode him right."

"Hey, what's wrong with Derek?" Ben asked, walking the colt in circles.

Derek was bent over, holding his stomach, the orange twine in his hand. Laughing convulsively, he tried to talk.

"Oh, man, I'm sorry, haha...I thought it was just hanging in his tail, but...oh dear, hahaha...he must have eaten it with his hay, and then it came part way out...oh man, haha...I jerked it right out of him...no wonder he bucked...I'm sorry, Ben!"

By then they were all bent over laughing, wiping tears from their eyes. Ben finally pulled the colt up between Pete and Fred.

"I can't believe what just happened. I didn't come off, and I wasn't even scared!"

Fred grinned. "That's because you relaxed and melted into that saddle, just like I've been telling you."

"Naw," argued Pete, "it's that saddle I gave you. I told you it was a good one."

"Actually," Ben said in amazement, "it was kind of fun!"

Adjusting his hat brim, he glanced over at the pen with the two colts.

Hmmm. Maybe I COULD ride them if they bucked.

Ranching Terms & Cowboy Slang

A-fork saddle The buckaroo-style saddle, with a wide wooden horn for roping, is called an "A-fork" or "slick fork." Viewed from the front, it is narrow at the top and slopes down like the letter "A," unlike a "swell fork" saddle, which swells or bulges out at the top. (See www.western-saddle-guide.com/swell-fork-saddle.html) Designed for comfort of horse and rider on the all-day rides required on huge Great Basin ranches, it evolved from the Mexican saddle of the 1800's.

alfalfa A leafy green crop often grown for hay. To turn alfalfa into hay, it must be cut, partly dried, and made into bales.

alley A long narrow passageway next to a set of corrals. Each corral's gate opens into the alley.

ATV All Terrain Vehicle, also known as a four-wheeler or a quad.

bag balm Lanolin ointment for cows' udders, also frequently used for human and animal cuts and sores.

bale Hay that has been compressed and tied into a rectangular shape. Regular bales, or small bales, are about three to four feet long and may weigh from 80 pounds to 130 pounds. Big bales can be about six feet long and weigh about a ton. There are also big round bales.

bale wagon or **harobed** (pronounced HARROW-bed) A machine for picking up rectangular bales from the field and stacking them. Harobed is the name of the inventor's daughter spelled backward (Deborah).

baler A tractor-like machine or a machine pulled by a tractor that picks up the cut and dried alfalfa, packs it tightly into bales, and ties it with twine or wire.

barb wire Barbed wire is a type of steel fencing wire with sharp barbs at intervals along the strand of wire. Often called barb wire or bobwire.

Basque (pronounced "bask") A descendant of a population group from the Pyrenees mountains on the border of France and Spain, many of whom settled in the inter-mountain West and became active in the sheep and cattle industries.

bay A reddish-brown horse with black legs and black mane and tail (also referred to as black points).

blow his plug Come unglued, blow up, explode.

bosal (pronounced bow-ZAL) A true hackamore, as opposed to a mechanical hackamore with metal parts. It consists of a braided noseband, usually of rawhide, hung from a light headstall (called a hanger), with a heel knot under the horse's chin where the mecate reins (usually horsehair) are attached. The bosal is generally the training stage between the snaffle and the bit. Sometimes horses are started in the bosal.

brand (noun) An identifying mark put on cattle or horses. It is applied quickly with a hot branding iron, leaving a permanent mark on the skin, like a tattoo. Each ranch not only has its own registered brand, but a particular location for its brand—left shoulder, right hip, left side, etc.

brand (verb) To rope calves and drag them to the branding fire where the heated branding irons are waiting. One rider ropes the head and another comes along and ropes the hind feet. The rider holds the reins and the coils of his lass rope in his left hand and throws the loop with his right hand. His horse must handle quietly and respond to leg pressure because the rider needs to position him to get the best possible shot with his loop. The horse must be able to calmly pull a bawling calf and not be bothered by commotion and ropes all around him because several pairs of ropers may be roping at the same time. Each horse and rider must work carefully to keep others from getting tangled in the ropes.

bridle A piece of equipment made of leather straps that goes over the horse's head and holds the bit in the horse's mouth. The reins are attached to the bit.

buckaroo A type of cowboy; from the Spanish term *vaquero*. A term most commonly used in the intermountain region of the West, known as the Great Basin—mainly California, Nevada, southern Idaho, and eastern Oregon. *Vaca* means "cow" in Spanish; *vaquero* means "vaca-worker" or "cow-worker." Vaquero became "bukera" (buh-KER-uh), then "buckaroo." Vaqueros came from early

California in the days of the missions, developing a slow, gentle way of handling cattle and horses, skillfully using long ropes or riatas and dallying to keep from jerking the cattle. Buckaroos are known for their hand-crafted equipment. Texas cowboys tend to run cattle faster, use short ropes, and tie hard and fast. Clothing and saddle styles may also vary between cowboys and Great Basin buckaroos.

build a loop To build a loop in a lass rope, you hold the coiled rope in your left hand and with your right hand on the hondoo, turn and shake out the end with the hondoo to make that coil into a bigger loop. With a flick of your right wrist, you turn it and whip the rope, feeding out coils with your left hand, so more rope slides through the hondoo until you have a loop the size you want.

bull A male member of the cattle (bovine) family. A mature female is a cow; a young female is a heifer. A young male is a calf, but calf can refer to any young animal, male or female. Plural of calf is calves.

bunkhouse A building on a ranch where single cowboys live.

cantle The rear part of the saddle seat that curves upward.

chaps (pronounced "shaps") From the Spanish term *chapareras* or *chaparajos*. Leather leggings worn over jeans, to protect the legs and clothing from brush. Often with fringe along the edge. Full-length chaps are called shotguns and are worn mainly in cold weather. In warm weather, cowboys often wear short chaps, called chinks, which come to the knee or below. Chaps also give the rider a more secure seat in the saddle; leather leggings against a leather saddle are not as slippery as jeans against leather.

Cheyenne roll A roll of leather that extends back and down off the top of the cantle, making a good hand-hold to help stay in the saddle. Thought to be named after the town where it was invented.

cinch From the Spanish *cincha* meaning "belt." Made of webbing, leather or other materials, it goes around the horse's belly to hold the saddle in place, with large rings on each end that the latigos are attached to. Some saddles also have a back cinch, a wide leather strap attached to the saddle just behind the stirrups. This helps stabilize the saddle, especially when roping cattle.

colt A young horse, especially a young horse that is not yet fully trained. A horse is considered mature around 5-7 years of age, by which time it is no longer referred to as a colt. Also may refer technically to a young male horse, whereas a young female is a filly.

concho An ornamental shell-shaped silver disk.

cowboss The head cowboy on a ranch employing a number of cowboys, somewhat like a foreman. If the ranch also engages in farming and employs farm help, there might also be a farmboss. These two would report directly to the owner, or if the ranch is run by a ranch manager, to that person.

cow camp A primitive one-room cabin in the mountains or out in the desert, far from the ranch headquarters but located on its leased public land, where one or more cowboys may stay for periods of time. It may also have a set of corrals. Many ranches have an "open door policy" on their cow camps: anyone in the area may stay in them in a pinch, provided they replace the supplies and firewood they use.

crowhop A mild form of bucking, usually a series of little short jumps, not hard to ride. Instead of kicking the hind feet up and out, the feet stay down, the head goes down, and the back is arched.

cutting (of alfalfa hay) When alfalfa is swathed (cut) to be made into hay, it is partly dried, raked once to turn it over for even drying, and then baled, removed from the field, and stored in a stack in a stack yard. That is one cutting of hay. The alfalfa plants are then watered, continue to grow, and 4-6 weeks later, are again swathed, raked, baled, and stacked. That is another cutting of hay. In cold climates and high elevations, 2-3 cuttings are common in one growing season. In warmer climates, 8-10 cuttings are possible.

dally From the Spanish term *de la vuerto* meaning "to go around." To go around the horn with a rope one or more times. Because the rope isn't tied down hard and fast, the dallies can be "slipped" or let run on the horn for easier and more humane handling of cattle.

discing Working up a field with a disc. A disc is a large, heavy implement with blades that cut into the ground, turn the soil, and loosen it so seeds can take root. It is pulled behind a tractor.

filly A young female horse.

flake (of hay) When alfalfa is mechanically fed into a baler, the baler's plunger compresses the hay each time it takes a stroke. Each stroke forms a tightly packed chunk of hay—a flake. When the bale is broken open for feeding, it can be easily pulled apart in flakes, each about four inches thick.

fork (verb) To straddle a horse; your legs are like the tines of a fork on each side. A cowboy that can stay in the saddle, no matter how rank the horse, is considered pretty "fork-ed," pronounced as two syllables.

gelding A male horse that has been castrated, a process in which the sex glands are removed. Colts are generally gelded by the age of two. A gelding has a calmer, more even disposition than a stud (an intact male, also called a stallion, used for breeding and sometimes also for riding).

gimping Walking with a limp.

gooseneck trailer A stock trailer with a front end that extends over the pickup bed. Its hitch attaches in the middle of the bed, over the axle. Because of this arrangement, it pulls better than bumper-pull trailers. Most are big enough to hold four or more horses or cows.

green Inexperienced. May refer to an unstarted horse, or to a young horse that is being ridden but isn't very far along in his training yet. May also refer to an inexperienced rider.

hackamore See **bosal**.

halter A loose bitless headgear of rope or leather, to which a lead rope can be attached so that a horse may be led or tied.

halter break To put a halter on a horse and teach it to accept being led and tied up. The horse generally struggles against the rope a bit until it realizes it cannot gain its freedom by pulling against the rope. Once a horse has been halter broke, it can be easily led or tied.

hand Someone who's pretty good help, particularly around a ranch or with a horse. Examples: "He'll never make a hand," or, "He's a pretty fair hand with a horse." Hand is also a unit of measure—four inches. Horses are measured in hands, not feet or inches. Their height is measured at the withers, the bony hump where the neck meets the back at the top of the shoulder blades. For example, the size range of the average ranch horse might be: 15, 15-1 (15 hands and 1 inch), 15-2, 15-3, 16.

hard mouth A mouth that resists the rider and does not readily give to the bit/reins/rider's hands, resulting in a horse that is difficult to direct and control.

harobed See **bale wagon**.

have your hammer cocked Be ready for whatever happens.

hay Partly dried grass or alfalfa that is usually formed into bales for long-term storage.

haying The process of growing and making hay.

headed In cattle roping: roped around the neck.

headstall The part of a bridle consisting of leather straps that go over and around the horse's head; it does not include the bit or reins.

hondoo From the Spanish term *hondo* meaning "deep." Also called hondo or honda. A metal, plastic or braided leather oblong ring at the end of a rope through which the rope is passed to make a loop. It may also be a loop braided into the end of the rope.

hon-yock As used here, a playful putdown implying a redneck, hillbilly, or someone a bit "dumb."

ironed out Bucked off, flattened.

kink in his tail A horse that is tense might hold his tail tensely clamped against its hindquarters. This causes the bony tip to stick out of the tail hairs a bit. Also called having a "fork" in its tail.

lass rope Another word for lasso. More often just called a rope. Buckaroos generally refer to a rope or lass rope; Texas cowboys would be more apt to say lasso or lariat.

lasso (pronounced lass-sue) From the Spanish term *lazo* meaning "length of line." A particular type of stiff narrow rope used for roping animals. A large loop is formed, swung, and thrown over the head or around the feet. Also called lariat, from the Spanish, *la riata*, meaning "the rope." Lasso and lariat are terms seldom used by buckaroos.

latigo From the Spanish term *latigo* meaning "the whip." A long leather strap that attaches the cinch ring to the rigging ring on each side of a western saddle. The cinch hangs from the right latigo. To cinch up, the cinch is brought under the horse's belly and up to the left latigo, which is wrapped snugly several times and either buckled or tied.

lead mare The mare that serves as the leader in a herd.

lead rope A rope attached to the halter for leading and tying.

lope is synonymous with canter, a three-beat gait. Gallop is a four-beat gait, the horse's fastest gait. Western riders might refer to gallop as a hard lope or a dead run.

mare A female horse, especially a mature female.

McCarty An Americanization of the term "mecate," often used by buckaroos in the Great Basin.
mucked out Bucked off hard and slammed into the dirt.

mecate Spanish. A set of braided rope or horsehair reins, made of one long rope, with 10-12 feet left for a lead rope, attached to the saddle or the rider's belt.

on the hook A cow that is "on the hook" is mad, slinging her horns to try to hook someone or something. When applied to a person, the connotation is "grouchy" or "mad."

onry Ornery.

outfit As used here, a ranch. Could also mean a cowboy's gear—the stuff he owns.

owl-headed Thick-skulled, dense, not too bright—with big blank staring eyes like an owl.

potlikker A mongrel dog, but also a term that expresses a low opinion of something, or just a meaningless but colorful name to call someone.

public lands When Nevada became a state, Congress attached a condition: Nevada must give up ownership of all land which was not privately owned at that time—87% of Nevada's land. Although controlled by the government, this land is for public use. For the first 70 years of Nevada's statehood, it was free grazing land. But problems developed. Some stockmen put too many animals on the range and let them overgraze it. The federal government had to step in and solve these problems.

In 1934 the Taylor Grazing Act was passed. Grazing districts were established. Rules and regulations followed. Ranchers had to apply for grazing permits and pay grazing fees. Grazing permits are handled by the U.S. Forest Service and the BLM (Bureau of Land Management). These agencies limit the number and type of livestock on each allotment and the length of time they can graze there.

The BLM, which was formed in 1947, manages 261 million acres of public lands, which are located mostly in 12 western states. Today there is much controversy over the use of public lands by ranchers. Some ecologists and government bureaucrats say cattle damage public lands. Ranchers claim they can't afford to raise cattle without the use of public lands. Studies show that grazing actually improves the health of rangelands.

riata From the Spanish term la *riata*, meaning "the rope." Also spelled "reata." A lasso made of braided rawhide, generally 65-80 feet long, sometimes even 90 feet. Often used in the intermountain region where the Spanish vaquero influence is still felt (mainly California, Nevada, southern Idaho, eastern Oregon).

roan A horse of red, black or brown coloring, lightened with scattered white hairs, and with darker head and legs.

rope strap A long strap attached just below the right side of the horn. It is wrapped several times around the coiled rope, then around the horn, then buckled tightly. A snugly buckled rope makes a good hand-hold if a horse bucks.

roundpen A round corral often used for starting horses, maybe 50-70 feet across.

run mustangs To chase and catch wild horses.

scatter Take off unexpectedly.

slip a dally After taking a dally around the horn, to let the rope run around the horn a little.

snaffle/snaffle bit A snaffle bit is a mild jointed bit that works on the corners of the horse's lips rather than the inside of the mouth. It is generally used on young horses before they are introduced to a bit and is generally used with two hands on the reins. A bit works on the mouth, has shanks on the side that exert leverage, and is used one-handed. A horse that goes in a bit is said to be "in the bridle." A horse may be "started in the bridle," or if it well-trained and highly responsive to the bridle, is said to be "bridled," "straight up in the bridle," "finished" or is referred to as a "bridle horse." Many cowboys routinely ride their horses in the snaffle regardless of the horse's age or stage of training because it is so easy on the mouth. When talking about types of bits, "bit" does not refer to the snaffle, but rather a leverage bit. However, if you are putting the snaffle in the horse's mouth, you would say you are putting the bit in his mouth.

soft mouth A mouth that easily and willingly yields to the bit/reins/rider's hands, resulting in a horse that is easy to direct and control.

sorrel A reddish-orange horse, usually with mane and tail of the same color as its coat.

spade bit A bit often used in the Great Basin by buckaroos that follow the tradition of the vaqueros. It is used only after the horse is advanced enough to respond to very slight signals of the rider's hands and body.

spooky Describes a horse that spooks easily—that startles or jumps at any little noise, movement, or unusual object.

spurs From the Spanish term *la espuela*. Metal prods strapped to the heel of the boot. They vary from short to long. They usually have a rowel—a spinning disk with sharp or dull points. Spurs are often inlaid with silver, and spur straps are often stamped with intricate designs.

start a colt To teach a green (unstarted) colt to accept handling by a human, to accept a halter, to tie, to accept a saddle and rider, and to begin his training under saddle.

stock saddle A large, heavy western-style saddle used for working livestock.

stock trailer A trailer for hauling livestock, usually larger than the common two-horse trailer.

swather A piece of farm equipment used for cutting hay. It may be a tractor-like machine with cutting blades on the front, or it may be an implement pulled behind a tractor.

tack room A room in or near a barn or stable where saddles and other tack (horse equipment) are kept.

tie rack Hitching rail, where you tie horses to saddle them.

vapor lock What happens when an engine stalls because it doesn't get enough oxygen. By implication, to quit breathing.

vaqueros The traditional Spanish/Mexican style cowboys. With their traditions of fine horsemanship, they became the symbol of the American West, later called "buckaroos" and then "cowboys." See "buckaroo."

wad up To tense up and prepare to buck.

whipper snapper A lively, mischievous or presumptuous young person; often said jokingly.

white-faced cattle A common term for Hereford cattle, which are usually red with white faces. They are raised for beef.

wildrag A large neckerchief or scarf of shiny, satiny or silky material, usually at least three feet square. It is folded in half from two farthest corners, forming a triangle, then wrapped twice around the neck and tied in a knot. A common item of buckaroo clothing, especially in cold weather.

windy An exaggerated, boastful story; full of "hot air."

woss-hoffer A horse that throws a bucking, squealing fit.

yay-hoo A friendly joshing put-down.